Francis Parkman

Historic Handbook of Northern Tour

Francis Parkman

Historic Handbook of Northern Tour

ISBN/EAN: 9783337329655

Printed in Europe, USA, Canada, Australia, Japan

Cover: Foto ©Andreas Hilbeck / pixelio.de

More available books at **www.hansebooks.com**

HISTORIC HANDBOOK

OF THE

NORTHERN TOUR.

LAKES GEORGE AND CHAMPLAIN; NIAGARA;
MONTREAL; QUEBEC.

BY

FRANCIS PARKMAN.

BOSTON:
LITTLE, BROWN, AND COMPANY.
1899.

THIS book is a group of narratives of the most striking events of our colonial history connected with the principal points of interest to the tourist visiting Canada and the northern borders of the United States.

The narratives are drawn, with the addition of explanatory passages, from " The Conspiracy of Pontiac," " Pioneers of France in the New World," " The Jesuits in North America," " Count Frontenac," and " Montcalm and Wolfe."

BOSTON, 1 April, 1885.

CONTENTS.

LAKE GEORGE AND LAKE CHAMPLAIN.

NIAGARA.

MONTREAL.

QUEBEC.

LAKE GEORGE AND LAKE CHAMPLAIN.

1

DISCOVERY OF LAKE CHAMPLAIN.

THIS beautiful lake owes its name to Samuel de Champlain, the founder of Quebec. In 1609, long before the Pilgrim Fathers landed at Plymouth, he joined a band of Huron and Algonquin warriors on an expedition against their enemies, the Iroquois, since known as the Five Nations of New York. While gratifying his own love of adventure, he expected to make important geographical discoveries.

After a grand war dance at the infant settlement of Quebec, the allies set out together. Champlain was in a boat, carrying, besides himself, eleven men, chief among whom were one Marais and a pilot named La Routte, all armed with the arquebuse, a species of firearm shorter than the musket, and therefore better fitted for the woods.

They ascended the St. Lawrence and entered the Richelieu, which forms the outlet of Lake Champlain. Here, to Champlain's great disappointment, he found his farther progress barred by the rapids at Chambly, though the Indians had assured him that his boat could pass all the way unobstructed. He told them that though they had deceived him, he would not abandon them, sent Marais with the boat and most of the men back to Quebec, and, with two who offered to follow him, prepared to go on in the Indian canoes.

The warriors lifted their canoes from the water, and in long procession through the forest, under the flickering sun and shade, bore them on their shoulders around the rapids to the smooth stream above. Here the chiefs made a muster of their forces, counting twenty-four canoes and sixty warriors. All embarked again, and advanced once more, by marsh, meadow, forest, and scattered islands, then full of game, for it was an uninhabited land, the war-path and battle-ground of hostile tribes. The warriors observed a certain system in their advance. Some were in front as a vanguard; others formed the main body; while an equal number were in the forests on the flanks and rear, hunting for the subsistence of the whole; for, though they had a provision of parched maize pounded into meal, they kept it for use when, from the vicinity of the enemy, hunting should become impossible.

Still the canoes advanced, the river widening as they went. Great islands appeared, leagues in extent: Isle à la Motte, Long Island, Grande Isle. Channels where ships might float and broad reaches of expanding water stretched between them, and Champlain entered the lake which preserves his name to posterity. Cumberland Head was passed, and from the opening of the great channel between Grande Isle and the main, he could look forth on the wilderness sea. Edged with woods, the tranquil flood spread southward beyond the sight. Far on the left, the forest ridges of the Green Mountains were heaved against the sun, patches of snow still glistening on their tops; and on the right rose the Adirondacks, haunts in these later years of amateur sportsmen from counting-rooms or college halls, nay, of adventurous beauty, with sketch-book and pencil. Then the Iroquois made them their hunting-ground; and beyond, in the valleys of the Mohawk, the Onondaga, and the Genesee, stretched the long line of their five cantons and palisaded towns.

The progress of the party was becoming dangerous. They changed their mode of advance, and moved only in the night. All day, they lay close in the depth of the forest, sleeping, lounging, smoking tobacco of their own raising, and beguiling the hours, no doubt, with the shallow banter and obscene jesting with which knots of Indians are wont to amuse their leisure. At twilight they embarked again, paddling their cautious way till the eastern sky began to redden. Their goal was the rocky promontory where Fort Ticonderoga was long afterward built. Thence, they would pass the outlet of Lake George, and launch their canoes again on that Como of the wilderness, whose waters, limpid as a fountain-head, stretched far southward between their flanking mountains. Landing at the future site of Fort William Henry, they would carry their canoes through the forest to the River Hudson, and descending it, attack, perhaps, some outlying town of the Mohawks. In the next century this chain of lakes and rivers became the grand highway of savage and civilized war, a bloody debatable ground linked to memories of momentous conflicts.

The allies were spared so long a progress. On the morning of the twenty-ninth of July, after paddling all night, they hid as usual in the forest on the western shore, not far from Crown Point. The warriors stretched themselves to their slumbers, and Champlain, after walking for a time through the surrounding woods, returned to take his repose on a pile of spruce-boughs. Sleeping, he dreamed a dream, wherein he beheld the Iroquois drowning in the lake; and, essaying to rescue them, he was told by his Algonquin friends that they were good for nothing and had better be left to their fate. Now, he had been daily beset, on awakening, by his superstitious allies, eager to learn about his dreams; and, to this moment, his unbroken slumbers had failed to furnish the desired prognostics. The announcement of this auspicious vision filled the crowd with joy, and at nightfall they embarked, flushed with anticipated victories.

It was ten o'clock in the evening, when they descried dark objects in motion on the lake before them. These were a flotilla of Iroquois canoes, heavier and slower than theirs, for they were made of oak or elm bark. Each party saw the other, and the mingled war-cries pealed over the darkened water. The Iroquois, who were near the shore, having no stomach for an aquatic battle, landed, and, making night hideous with their clamors, began to barricade themselves. Champlain could see them in the woods, laboring like beavers, hacking down trees with iron axes taken from the Canadian tribes in war, and with stone hatchets of their own making. The allies remained on the lake, a bowshot from the hostile barricade, their canoes made fast together by poles lashed across. All night, they danced with as much vigor as the frailty of their vessels would permit, their throats making amends for the enforced restraint of their limbs. It was agreed on both sides that the fight should be deferred till daybreak; but meanwhile a commerce of abuse, sarcasm, menace, and boasting gave unceasing exercise to the lungs and fancy of the combatants, — "much," says Champlain, "like the besiegers and besieged in a beleaguered town."

As day approached, he and his two followers put on the light armor of the time. Champlain wore the

CHAMPLAIN'S FIGHT WITH THE IROQUOIS.

doublet and long hose then in vogue. Over the doublet
he buckled on a breastplate, and probably a back-piece,
while his thighs were protected by *cuisses* of steel, and
his head by a plumed casque. Across his shoulder hung
the strap of his bandoleer, or ammunition-box; at his
side was his sword, and in his hand his arquebuse, which
he had loaded with four balls. Such was the equipment
of this ancient Indian-fighter, whose exploits date eleven
years before the landing of the Puritans at Plymouth,
and sixty-six years before King Philip's War.

Each of the three Frenchmen was in a separate canoe,
and, as it grew light, they kept themselves hidden,
either by lying at the bottom, or covering themselves
with an Indian robe. The canoes approached the shore,
and all landed without opposition at some distance from
the Iroquois, whom they presently could see filing out of
their barricade, tall, strong men, some two hundred in
number, of the boldest and fiercest warriors of North
America. They advanced through the forest with a
steadiness which excited the admiration of Champlain.
Among them could be seen several chiefs, made con-
spicuous by their tall plumes. Some bore shields of wood
and hide, and some were covered with a kind of armor
made of tough twigs interlaced with a vegetable fibre
supposed by Champlain to be cotton.

The allies, growing anxious, called with loud cries
for their champion, and opened their ranks that he
might pass to the front. He did so, and, advancing
before his red companions-in-arms, stood revealed to
the astonished gaze of the Iroquois, who, beholding the
warlike apparition in their path, stared in mute amazement. But his arquebuse was levelled; the report
startled the woods, a chief fell dead, and another by
his side rolled among the bushes. Then there rose

from the allies a yell, which, says Champlain, would
have drowned a thunder-clap, and the forest was full of
whizzing arrows.   For a moment, the Iroquois stood
firm and sent back their arrows lustily; but when another and another gunshot came from the thickets on
their flank, they broke and fled in uncontrollable terror.
Swifter than hounds, the allies tore through the bushes
in pursuit.   Some of the Iroquois were killed; more
were taken.   Camp, canoes, provisions, all were abandoned, and many weapons flung down in the panic
flight.   The arquebuse had done its work.   The victory was complete.

The victors made a prompt retreat from the scene of
their triumph.   Three or four days brought them to
the mouth of the Richelieu.   Here they separated; the
Hurons and Algonquins made for the Ottawa, their
homeward route, each with a share of prisoners for
future torments.   At parting they invited Champlain
to visit their towns and aid them again in their wars,
— an invitation which this paladin of the woods failed
not to accept.

Thus did New France rush into collision with the
redoubted warriors of the Five Nations.   Here was the
beginning, in some measure doubtless the cause, of a
long suite of murderous conflicts, bearing havoc and
flame to generations yet unborn.   Champlain had in-
vaded the tiger's den; and now, in smothered fury, the
patient savage would lie biding his day of blood.

DISCOVERY OF LAKE GEORGE.

IT was thirty-three years since Champlain had first attacked the Iroquois. They had nursed their wrath for more than a generation, and at length their hour was come. The Dutch traders at Fort Orange, now Albany, had supplied them with firearms. The Mohawks, the most easterly of the Iroquois nations, had, among their seven or eight hundred warriors, no less than three hundred armed with the arquebuse. They were masters of the thunderbolts which, in the hands of Champlain, had struck terror into their hearts.

In the early morning of the second of August, 1642, twelve Huron canoes were moving slowly along the northern shore of the expansion of the St. Lawrence known as the Lake of St. Peter. There were on board about forty persons, including four Frenchmen, one of them being the Jesuit, Isaac Jogues. During the last autumn he, with Father Charles Raymbault, had passed along the shore of Lake Huron northward, entered the strait through which Lake Superior discharges itself, pushed on as far as the Sault Sainte Marie, and preached the Faith to two thousand Ojibwas, and other Algonquins there assembled. He was now on his return from a far more perilous errand. The Huron mission was in a state of destitution. There was need of clothing for the priests, of vessels for the altars, of bread and wine for the eucharist, of writing materials, — in short, of everything; and, early in the summer of the present year, Jogues had descended to Three Rivers and Quebec with the Huron traders, to procure the necessary supplies. He had accomplished his task, and was on his way back to the mission. With him were a few Huron converts, and among them a noted Christian chief, Eustache Ahatsistari. Others of the party were in course of instruction for baptism; but the greater part were heathen, whose canoes were deeply laden with the proceeds of their bargains with the French fur-traders.

Jogues sat in one of the leading canoes. He was born at Orleans in 1607, and was thirty-five years of age. His oval face and the delicate mould of his features indicated a modest, thoughtful, and refined nature. He was constitutionally timid, with a sensitive conscience and great religious susceptibilities. He was a finished scholar, and might have gained a literary reputation; but he had chosen another career, and one for which he seemed but ill fitted. Physically, however, he was well matched with his work; for, though his frame was slight, he was so active, that none of the Indians could surpass him in running.

With him were two young men, René Goupil and Guillaume Couture, *donnés* of the mission, — that is to say, laymen who, from a religious motive and without pay, had attached themselves to the service of the Jesuits. Goupil had formerly entered upon the Jesuit novitiate at Paris, but failing health had obliged him to leave it. As soon as he was able, he came to Canada, offered his services to the Superior of the mission, was employed for a time in the humblest offices, and afterwards became an attendant at the hospital. At length, to his delight, he received permission to go up to the Hurons, where the surgical skill which he had acquired was greatly needed; and he was now on his way thither. His companion, Couture, was a man of intelligence and vigor, and of a character equally disinterested. Both were, like Jogues, in the foremost canoes; while the fourth Frenchman was with the unconverted Hurons, in the rear.

The twelve canoes had reached the western end of the Lake of St. Peter, where it is filled with innumerable islands. The forest was close on their right, they kept near the shore to avoid the current, and the shallow water before them was covered with a dense growth of tall bulrushes. Suddenly the silence was frightfully broken. The war-whoop rose from among the rushes, mingled with the reports of guns and the whistling of bullets; and several Iroquois canoes, filled with warriors, pushed out from their concealment, and bore down upon Jogues and his companions. The Hurons in the rear were seized with a shameful panic. They leaped ashore; left canoes, baggage, and weapons; and fled into the woods. The French and the Christian Hurons made fight for a time; but when they saw another fleet of canoes approaching from the opposite shores or islands, they lost heart, and those escaped who could. Goupil was seized amid triumphant yells, as were also several of the Huron converts. Jogues sprang into the bulrushes, and might have escaped; but when he saw Goupil and the neophytes in the clutches of the Iroquois, he had no heart to abandon them, but came out from his hiding-place, and gave himself up to the astonished victors. A few of them had remained to guard the prisoners; the rest were chasing the fugitives. Jogues mastered his agony, and began to baptize those of the captive converts who needed baptism.

Couture had eluded pursuit; but when he thought of

Jogues and of what perhaps awaited him, he resolved to share his fate, and, turning, retraced his steps. As he approached, five Iroquois ran forward to meet him; and one of them snapped his gun at his breast, but it missed fire. In his confusion and excitement, Couture fired his own piece, and laid the savage dead. The remaining four sprang upon him, stripped off all his clothing, tore away his finger-nails with their teeth, gnawed his fingers with the fury of famished dogs, and thrust a sword through one of his hands. Jogues broke from his guards, and, rushing to his friend, threw his arms about his neck. The Iroquois dragged him away, beat him with their fists and war-clubs till he was senseless, and, when he revived, lacerated his fingers with their teeth, as they had done those of Couture. Then they turned upon Goupil, and treated him with the same ferocity. The Huron prisoners were left for the present unharmed. More of them were brought in every moment, till at length the number of captives amounted in all to twenty-two, while three Hurons had been killed in the fight and pursuit. The Iroquois, about seventy in number, now embarked with their prey: but not until they had knocked on the head an old Huron, whom Jogues, with his mangled hands, had just baptized, and who refused to leave the place. Then, under a burning sun, they crossed to the spot on which the town of Sorel now stands, at the mouth of the River Richelieu, where they encamped.

Their course was southward, up the River Richelieu and Lake Champlain; thence, by way of Lake George, to the Mohawk towns. The pain and fever of their wounds, and the clouds of mosquitoes, which they could not drive off, left the prisoners no peace by day nor sleep by night. On the eighth day, they learned that a large Iroquois war-party, on their way to Canada, were near at hand ; and they soon approached their camp, on a small island near the southern end of Lake Champlain. The warriors, two hundred in number, saluted their victorious countrymen with volleys from their guns ; then, armed with clubs and thorny sticks, ranged themselves in two lines, between which the captives were compelled to pass up the side of a rocky hill. On the way, they were beaten with such fury, that Jogues, who was last in the line, fell powerless, drenched in blood and half dead. As the chief man among the French captives, he fared the worst. His hands were again mangled, and fire applied to his body ; while the Huron chief, Eustache, was subjected to tortures even more atrocious. When, at night, the exhausted sufferers tried to rest, the young warriors came to lacerate their wounds and pull out their hair and beards.

In the morning they resumed their journey. And now the lake narrowed to the semblance of a tranquil river. Before them was a woody mountain, close on their right a rocky promontory, and between these flowed a stream, the outlet of Lake George. On those rocks, more than a hundred years after, rose the ramparts of Ticonderoga. They landed, shouldered their canoes and baggage, took their way through the woods, passed the spot where the fierce Highlanders and the dauntless regiments of England breasted in vain the storm of lead and fire, and soon reached the shore where Abercrombie landed and Lord Howe fell. First of white men, Jogues and his companions gazed on the romantic lake that bears the name, not of its gentle discoverer, but of the dull Hanoverian king. Like a fair Naiad of the wilderness, it slumbered between the guardian mountains that breathe from crag and forest the stern poetry

of war. But all then was solitude; and the clang of
trumpets, the roar of cannon, and the deadly crack of
the rifle had never as yet awakened their angry echoes.[1]

Again the canoes were launched, and the wild flotilla
glided on its way, — now in the shadow of the heights,
now on the broad expanse, now among the devious channels of the narrows, beset with woody islets, where the
hot air was redolent of the pine, the spruce, and the
cedar, — till they neared that tragic shore, where, in
the following century, New England rustics baffled the
soldiers of Dieskau, where Montcalm planted his batteries, where the red cross waved so long amid the
smoke, and where at length the summer morning was
hideous with carnage, and an honored name was stained
with a memory of blood.

The Iroquois landed at or near the future site of Fort
William Henry, left their canoes, and, with their prisoners, began their march for the nearest Mohawk town.
Each bore his share of the plunder. Even Jogues,
though his lacerated hands were in a frightful condition
and his body covered with bruises, was forced to stagger
on with the rest under a heavy load. He with his
fellow-prisoners, and indeed the whole party, were half

[1] Lake George, according to Jogues, was called by the Mohawks
"Andiatarocte," or *Place where the Lake closes*. "Andiatarnque" is
found on a map of Sanson. Spofford, *Gazetteer of New York*, article
"Lake George," says that it was called "Canideri-oit," or *Tail of the
Lake*. Father Martin, in his notes on Bressani, prefixes to this name
that of "Horicon," but gives no original authority.

I have seen an old Latin map on which the name "Horiconi" is set
down as belonging to a neighboring tribe. This seems to be only a
misprint for "Horicoui," that is, "Irocoui," or "Iroquois." In an old
English map, prefixed to the rare tract, *A Treatise of New England*, the
"Lake of Hierocoyes" is laid down. The name "Horicon," as used by
Cooper in his *Last of the Mohicans*, has no sufficient historical foundation.
In 1646, the lake, as we shall see, was named "Lac St. Sacrement."

starved, subsisting chiefly on wild berries. They crossed the upper Hudson, and, in thirteen days after leaving the St. Lawrence, neared the wretched goal of their pilgrimage, a palisaded town, standing on a hill by the banks of the River Mohawk.

Such was the first recorded visit of white men to Lake George. In the Iroquois villages Jogues was subjected to the most frightful sufferings. His friend Goupil was murdered at his side, and he himself was saved as by miracle. At length, with the help of the Dutch of Albany, he made his escape and sailed for France; whence, impelled by religious enthusiasm, he returned to Canada and voluntarily set out again for the Iroquois towns, bent on saving the souls of those who had been the authors of his woes. Reaching the head of Lake George on Corpus Christi Day, 1646, he gave it the name of Lac St. Sacrement, by which it was ever after known to the French. Soon after his arrival the Iroquois killed him by the blow of a hatchet.

BATTLE OF LAKE GEORGE.

FOR more than a century after the death of Jogues, Lakes George and Champlain were the great route of war parties between Canada and the British Colonies. Courcelles came this way in 1666 to lay waste the Mohawk towns; and Mantet and Sainte-Hélène, in 1690, to destroy Schenectady in the dead of winter; while, in the next year, Major Schuyler took the same course as he advanced into Canada to retort the blow. Whenever there was war between France and England, these two lakes became the scene of partisan conflicts, in which the red men took part with the white, some as allies of the English, and some as allies of the French. When at length the final contest took place for the possession of the continent, the rival nations fiercely disputed the mastery of this great wilderness thoroughfare, and the borders of Lake George became the scene of noteworthy conflicts. The first of these was in 1755, the year of Braddock's defeat, when Shirley, governor of Massachusetts, set on foot an expedition for the capture of Crown Point, a fort which the French had built on Lake Champlain more than twenty years before.

In January, Shirley had proposed an attack on it to the Ministry; and in February, without waiting their reply, he laid the plan before his Assembly. They accepted it, and voted money for the pay and maintenance of twelve hundred men, provided the adjacent colonies

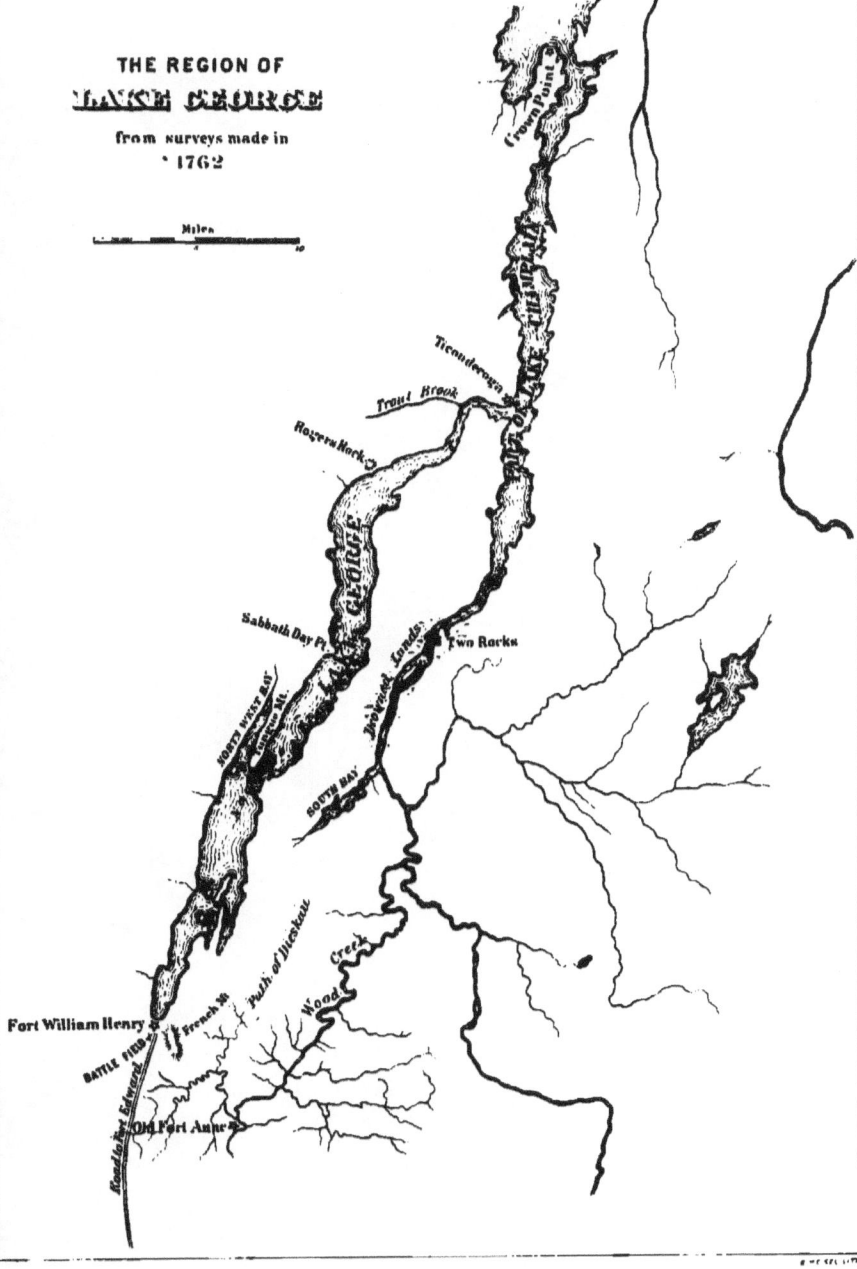

THE REGION OF

LAKE GEORGE

from surveys made in
1762

Miles

would contribute in due proportion. Massachusetts showed a military activity worthy of the reputation she had won. Forty-five hundred of her men, or one in eight of her adult males, volunteered to fight the French, and enlisted for the various expeditions, some in the pay of the province, and some in that of the King. It remained to name a commander for the Crown Point enterprise. Nobody had power to do so, for Braddock, the commander-in-chief, was not yet come; but that time might not be lost, Shirley, at the request of his Assembly, took the responsibility on himself. If he had named a Massachusetts officer, it would have roused the jealousy of the other New England colonies; and he therefore appointed William Johnson, of New York, thus gratifying that important province and pleasing the Five Nations, who at this time looked on Johnson with even more than usual favor. Hereupon, in reply to his request, Connecticut voted twelve hundred men, New Hampshire five hundred, and Rhode Island four hundred, all at their own charge; while New York, a little later, promised eight hundred more. When, in April, Braddock and the Council at Alexandria approved the plan and the commander, Shirley gave Johnson the commission of major-general of the levies of Massachusetts; and the governors of the other provinces contributing to the expedition gave him similar commissions for their respective contingents. Never did general take the field with authority so heterogeneous.

He had never seen service, and knew nothing of war. By birth he was Irish, of good family, being nephew of Admiral Sir Peter Warren, who, owning extensive wild lands on the Mohawk, had placed the young man in charge of them nearly twenty years before. Johnson was born to prosper. He had ambition, energy, an active

mind, a tall, strong person, a rough, jovial temper, and a
quick adaptation to his surroundings. He could drink
flip with Dutch boors, or Madeira with royal governors.
He liked the society of the great, would intrigue and flatter when he had an end to gain, and foil a rival without
looking too closely at the means ; but compared with
the Indian traders who infested the border, he was a
model of uprightness. He lived by the Mohawk in a
fortified house which was a stronghold against foes and
a scene of hospitality to friends, both white and red.
Here — for his tastes were not fastidious — presided for
many years a Dutch or German wench whom he finally
married ; and after her death a young Mohawk squaw
took her place. Over his neighbors, the Indians of the
Five Nations, and all others of their race with whom he
had to deal, he acquired a remarkable influence. He
liked them, adopted their ways, and treated them kindly
or sternly as the case required, but always with a justice
and honesty in strong contrast with the rascalities of
the commission of Albany traders who had lately managed their affairs, and whom they so detested that one
of their chiefs called them " not men, but devils."
Hence, when Johnson was made Indian superintendent
there was joy through all the Iroquois confederacy.
When, in addition, he was made a general, he assembled
the warriors in council to engage them to aid the
expedition.

This meeting took place at his own house, known as
Fort Johnson ; and as more than eleven hundred Indians appeared at his call, his larder was sorely taxed
to entertain them. The speeches were interminable.
Johnson, a master of Indian rhetoric, knew his audience
too well not to contest with them the palm of insufferable prolixity. The climax was reached on the fourth

day, and he threw down the war-belt. An Oneida chief took it up; Stevens, the interpreter, began the war-dance, and the assembled warriors howled in chorus. Then a tub of punch was brought in, and they all drank the King's health. They showed less alacrity, however, to fight his battles, and scarcely three hundred of them would take the war-path. Too many of their friends and relatives were enlisted for the French.

While the British colonists were preparing to attack Crown Point, the French of Canada were preparing to defend it. Duquesne, recalled from his post, had resigned the government to the Marquis de Vaudreuil, who had at his disposal the battalions of regulars that had sailed in the spring from Brest under Baron Dieskau. His first thought was to use them for the capture of Oswego; but letters of Braddock, found on the battle-field of the Monongahela, warned him of the design against Crown Point; while a reconnoitring party which had gone as far as the Hudson brought back news that Johnson's forces were already in the field. Therefore the plan was changed, and Dieskau was ordered to lead the main body of his troops, not to Lake Ontario, but to Lake Champlain. He passed up the Richelieu, and embarked in boats and canoes for Crown Point. The veteran knew that the foes with whom he had to deal were but a mob of countrymen. He doubted not of putting them to rout, and meant never to hold his hand till he had chased them back to Albany. "Make all haste," Vaudreuil wrote to him; "for when you return we shall send you to Oswego to execute our first design."

Johnson on his part was preparing to advance. In July about three thousand provincials were encamped near Albany, some on the "Flats" above the town, and some on the meadows below. Hither, too, came a swarm of Johnson's Mohawks,—warriors, squaws, and children. They adorned the General's face with war-paint, and he danced the war-dance; then with his sword he cut the first slice from the ox that had been roasted whole for their entertainment. "I shall be glad," wrote the surgeon of a New England regiment, "if they fight as eagerly as they ate their ox and drank their wine."

Above all things the expedition needed promptness; yet everything moved slowly. Five popular legislatures controlled the troops and the supplies. Connecticut had refused to send her men till Shirley promised that her commanding officer should rank next to Johnson. The whole movement was for some time at a deadlock because the five governments could not agree about their contributions of artillery and stores. The New Hampshire regiment had taken a short cut for Crown Point across the wilderness of Vermont; but had been recalled in time to save them from probable destruction. They were now with the rest in the camp at Albany, in such distress for provisions that a private subscription was proposed for their relief.

Johnson's army, crude as it was, had in it good material. Here was Phineas Lyman, of Connecticut, second in command, once a tutor at Yale College, and more recently a lawyer,—a raw soldier, but a vigorous and brave one; Colonel Moses Titcomb, of Massachusetts, who had fought with credit at Louisbourg; and Ephraim Williams, also colonel of a Massachusetts regiment, a tall and portly man, who had been a captain in the last war, member of the General Court, and deputy-sheriff. He made his will in the camp at Albany, and left a legacy to found the school which has since become Williams College. His relative, Stephen Williams, was chaplain of his regiment, and his brother Thomas was

its surgeon. Seth Pomeroy, gunsmith at Northampton,
who, like Titcomb, had seen service at Louisbourg, was
its lieutenant-colonel. He had left a wife at home, an
excellent matron, to whom he was continually writing
affectionate letters, mingling household cares with news
of the camp, and charging her to see that their eldest
boy, Seth, then in college at New Haven, did not run off
to the army. Pomeroy had with him his brother Daniel;
and this he thought was enough. Here, too, was a man
whose name is still a household word in New England,
— the sturdy Israel Putnam, private in a Connecticut
regiment: and another as bold as he, John Stark, lieutenant in the New Hampshire levies, and the future
victor of Bennington.

The soldiers were no soldiers, but farmers and farmers'
sons who had volunteered for the summer campaign.
One of the corps had a blue uniform faced with red.
The rest wore their daily clothing. Blankets had been
served out to them by the several provinces, but the
greater part brought their own guns; some under the
penalty of a fine if they came without them, and some
under the inducement of a reward. They had no bayonets, but carried hatchets in their belts as a sort of
substitute. At their sides were slung powder-horns, on
which, in the leisure of the camp, they carved quaint
devices with the points of their jack-knives. They came
chiefly from plain New England homesteads, — rustic
abodes, unpainted and dingy, with long well-sweeps,
capacious barns, rough fields of pumpkins and corn,
and vast kitchen chimneys, above which in winter hung
squashes to keep them from frost, and guns to keep
them from rust.

As to the manners and morals of the army there is
conflict of evidence. In some respects nothing could

be more exemplary. "Not a chicken has been stolen," says William Smith, of New York; while, on the other hand, Colonel Ephraim Williams writes to Colonel Israel Williams, then commanding on the Massachusetts frontier: "We are a wicked, profane army, especially the New York and Rhode Island troops. Nothing to be heard among a great part of them but the language of Hell. If Crown Point is taken, it will not be for our sakes, but for those good people left behind." There was edifying regularity in respect to form. Sermons twice a week, daily prayers, and frequent psalm-singing alternated with the much-needed military drill. "Prayers among us night and morning," writes Private Jonathan Caswell, of Massachusetts, to his father. "Here we lie, knowing not when we shall march for Crown Point; but I hope not long to tarry. Desiring your prayers to God for me as I am agoing to war, I am Your Ever Dutiful Son."

To Pomeroy and some of his brothers in arms it seemed that they were engaged in a kind of crusade against the myrmidons of Rome. "As you have at heart the Protestant cause," he wrote to his friend Israel Williams, "so I ask an interest in your prayers that the Lord of Hosts would go forth with us and give us victory over our unreasonable, encroaching, barbarous, murdering enemies."

Both Williams the surgeon and Williams the colonel chafed at the incessant delays. "The expedition goes on very much as a snail runs," writes the former to his wife; "it seems we may possibly see Crown Point this time twelve months." The Colonel was vexed because everything was out of joint in the department of trans-portation: wagoners mutinous for want of pay; ordnance stores, camp-kettles, and provisions left behind. "As to

rum," he complains, "it won't hold out nine weeks.
Things appear most melancholy to me." Even as he
was writing, a report came of the defeat of Braddock;
and, shocked at the blow, his pen traced the words: " The
Lord have mercy on poor New England!"

Johnson had sent four Mohawk scouts to Canada.
They returned on the twenty-first of August with the
report that the French were all astir with preparation,
and that eight thousand men were coming to defend
Crown Point. On this a council of war was called; and
it was resolved to send to the several colonies for
reinforcements. Meanwhile the main body had moved
up the river to the spot called the Great Carrying Place,
where Lyman had begun a fortified storehouse, which
his men called Fort Lyman, but which was afterwards
named Fort Edward. Two Indian trails led from this
point to the waters of Lake Champlain, one by way of
Lake George, and the other by way of Wood Creek.
There was doubt which course the army should take.
A road was begun to Wood Creek; then it was countermanded, and a party was sent to explore the path to
Lake George. "With submission to the general officers," Surgeon Williams again writes, " I think it a
very grand mistake that the business of reconnoitring
was not done months agone." It was resolved at last
to march for Lake George; gangs of axemen were sent
to hew out the way; and on the twenty-sixth two thousand men were ordered to the lake, while Colonel
Blanchard, of New Hampshire, remained with five hundred to finish and defend Fort Lyman.

The train of Dutch wagons, guarded by the homely
soldiery, jolted slowly over the stumps and roots of the
newly made road, and the regiments followed at their
leisure. The hardships of the way were not without

their consolations. The jovial Irishman who held the
chief command made himself very agreeable to the New
England officers. " We went on about four or five miles,"
says Pomeroy in his Journal, " then stopped, ate pieces of
broken bread and cheese, and drank some fresh lemon-
punch and the best of wine with General Johnson and
some of the field-officers." It was the same on the next
day. " Stopped about noon and dined with General
Johnson by a small brook under a tree; ate a good
dinner of cold boiled and roast venison; drank good
fresh lemon-punch and wine."

That afternoon they reached their destination, fourteen miles from Fort Lyman. The most beautiful lake
in America lay before them; then more beautiful than
now, in the wild charm of untrodden mountains and
virgin forests. " I have given it the name of Lake
George," wrote Johnson to the Lords of Trade, " not
only in honor of His Majesty, but to ascertain his un-
doubted dominion here." His men made their camp
on a piece of rough ground by the edge of the water,
pitching their tents among the stumps of the newly
felled trees. In their front was a forest of pitch-pine;
on their right, a marsh, choked with alders and swamp-
maples; on their left, the low hill where Fort George
was afterwards built; and at their rear, the lake. Little
was done to clear the forest in front, though it would
give excellent cover to an enemy. Nor did Johnson
take much pains to learn the movements of the French
in the direction of Crown Point, though he sent scouts
towards South Bay and Wood Creek. Every day stores
and bateaux, or flat boats, came on wagons from Fort
Lyman; and preparation moved on with the leisure that
had marked it from the first. About three hundred
Mohawks came to the camp, and were regarded by the

New England men as nuisances. On Sunday the gray-haired Stephen Williams preached to these savage allies a long Calvinistic sermon, which must have sorely perplexed the interpreter whose business it was to turn it into Mohawk; and in the afternoon young Chaplain Newell, of Rhode Island, expounded to the New England men the somewhat untimely text, " Love your enemies." On the next Sunday, September seventh, Williams preached again, this time to the whites from a text in Isaiah. It was a peaceful day, fair and warm, with a few light showers; yet not wholly a day of rest, for two hundred wagons came up from Fort Lyman, loaded with bateaux. After the sermon there was an alarm. An Indian scout came in about sunset, and reported that he had found the trail of a body of men moving from South Bay towards Fort Lyman. Johnson called for a volunteer to carry a letter of warning to Colonel Blanchard, the commander. A wagoner named Adams offered himself for the perilous service, mounted, and galloped along the road with the letter. Sentries were posted, and the camp fell asleep.

While Johnson lay at Lake George, Dieskau prepared a surprise for him. The German Baron had reached Crown Point at the head of three thousand five hundred and seventy-three men, regulars, Canadians, and Indians. He had no thought of waiting there to be attacked. The troops were told to hold themselves ready to move at a moment's notice. Officers — so ran the order — will take nothing with them but one spare shirt, one spare pair of shoes, a blanket, a bearskin, and provisions for twelve days; Indians are not to amuse themselves by taking scalps till the enemy is entirely defeated, since they can kill ten men in the time required to scalp one. Then Dieskau moved on, with nearly all his force, to

Carillon, or Ticonderoga, a promontory commanding
both the routes by which alone Johnson could advance,
that of Wood Creek and that of Lake George.

The Indian allies were commanded by Legardeur de
Saint-Pierre. These unmanageable warriors were a con-
stant annoyance to Dieskau, being a species of humanity
quite new to him. "They drive us crazy," he says,
"from morning till night. There is no end to their
demands. They have already eaten five oxen and as
many hogs, without counting the kegs of brandy they
have drunk. In short, one needs the patience of an
angel to get on with these devils; and yet one must
always force himself to seem pleased with them."

They would scarcely even go out as scouts. At last,
however, on the fourth of September, a reconnoitring
party came in with a scalp and an English prisoner
caught near Fort Lyman. He was questioned under the
threat of being given to the Indians for torture if he did
not tell the truth; but, nothing daunted, he invented a
patriotic falsehood; and thinking to lure his captors
into a trap, told them that the English army had fallen
back to Albany, leaving five hundred men at Fort
Lyman, which he represented as indefensible. Dieskau
resolved on a rapid movement to seize the place. At
noon of the same day, leaving a part of his force at
Ticonderoga, he embarked the rest in canoes and advanced along the narrow prolongation of Lake Champlain that stretched southward through the wilderness
to where the town of Whitehall now stands. He soon
came to a point where the lake dwindled to a mere canal,
while two mighty rocks, capped with stunted forests,
faced each other from the opposing banks. Here he
left an officer named Roquemaure with a detachment
of troops, and again advanced along a belt of quiet water

traced through the midst of a deep marsh, green at
that season with sedge and water-weeds, and known
to the English as the Drowned Lands. Beyond, on
either hand, crags feathered with birch and fir, or hills
mantled with woods, looked down on the long procession
of canoes. As they neared the site of Whitehall, a passage opened on the right, the entrance to a sheet of
lonely water slumbering in the shadow of woody mountains, and forming the lake then, as now, called South
Bay. They advanced to its head, landed where a small
stream enters it, left the canoes under a guard, and
began their march through the forest. They counted
in all two hundred and sixteen regulars of the battalions
of Languedoc and La Reine, six hundred and eighty-
four Canadians, and about six hundred Indians. Every
officer and man carried provisions for eight days in his
knapsack. They encamped at night by a brook, and in
the morning, after hearing Mass, marched again. The
evening of the next day brought them near the road that
led to Lake George. Fort Lyman was but three miles
distant. A man on horseback galloped by; it was
Adams, Johnson's unfortunate messenger. The Indians
shot him, and found the letter in his pocket. Soon
after, ten or twelve wagons appeared in charge of mutinous drivers, who had left the English camp without
orders. Several of them were shot, two were taken, and
the rest ran off. The two captives declared that, con-
trary to the assertion of the prisoner at Ticonderoga, a
large force lay encamped at the lake. The Indians now
held a council, and presently gave out that they would
not attack the fort, which they thought well supplied
with cannon, but that they were willing to attack the
camp at Lake George. Remonstrance was lost upon
them. Dieskau was not young, but he was daring to

rashness, and inflamed to emulation by the victory over Braddock. The enemy were reported greatly to outnumber him ; but his Canadian advisers had assured him that the English colony militia were the worst troops on the face of the earth. "The more there are," he said to the Canadians and Indians, "the more we shall kill ;" and in the morning the order was given to march for the lake.

They moved rapidly on through the waste of pines, and soon entered the rugged valley that led to Johnson's camp. On their right was a gorge where, shadowed in bushes, gurgled a gloomy brook ; and beyond rose the cliffs that buttressed the rocky heights of French Mountain, seen by glimpses between the boughs. On their left rose gradually the lower slopes of West Mountain. All was rock, thicket, and forest ; there was no open space but the road along which the regulars marched, while the Canadians and Indians pushed their way through the woods in such order as the broken ground would permit.

They were three miles from the lake, when their scouts brought in a prisoner who told them that a column of English troops was approaching. Dieskau's preparations were quickly made. While the regulars halted on the road, the Canadians and Indians moved to the front, where most of them hid in the forest along the slopes of West Mountain, and the rest lay close among the thickets on the other side. Thus, when the English advanced to attack the regulars in front, they would find themselves caught in a double ambush. No sight or sound betrayed the snare ; but behind every bush crouched a Canadian or a savage, with gun cocked and ears intent, listening for the tramp of the approaching column.

The wagoners who escaped the evening before had reached the camp about midnight, and reported that there was a war-party on the road near Fort Lyman. Johnson had at this time twenty-two hundred effective men, besides his three hundred Indians. He called a council of war in the morning, and a resolution was taken which can only be explained by a complete misconception as to the force of the French. It was determined to send out two detachments of five hundred men each, one towards Fort Lyman, and the other towards South Bay, the object being, according to Johnson, " to catch the enemy in their retreat." Hendrick, chief of the Mohawks, a brave and sagacious warrior, expressed his dissent after a fashion of his own. He picked up a stick and broke it; then he picked up several sticks, and showed that together they could not be broken. The hint was taken, and the two detachments were joined in one. Still the old savage shook his head. "If they are to be killed," he said, "they are too many; if they are to fight, they are too few." Nevertheless, he resolved to share their fortunes; and mounting on a gun-carriage, he harangued his warriors with a voice so animated, and gestures so expressive, that the New England officers listened in admiration, though they understood not a word. One difficulty remained. He was too old and fat to go afoot; but Johnson lent him a horse, which he bestrode, and trotted to the head of the column, followed by two hundred of his warriors as fast as they could grease, paint, and befeather themselves.

Captain Elisha Hawley was in his tent, finishing a letter which he had just written to his brother Joseph; and these were the last words: " I am this minute agoing out in company with five hundred men to see if we can intercept 'em in their retreat, or find their canoes in the Drowned Lands; and therefore must conclude this letter." He closed and directed it; and in an hour received his death-wound.

It was soon after eight o'clock when Ephraim Williams left the camp with his regiment, marched a little distance, and then waited for the rest of the detachment under Lieutenant-Colonel Whiting. Thus Dieskau had full time to lay his ambush. When Whiting came up, the whole moved on together, so little conscious of danger that no scouts were thrown out in front or flank; and, in full security, they entered the fatal snare. Before they were completely involved in it, the sharp eye of old Hendrick detected some sign of an enemy. At that instant, whether by accident or design, a gun was fired from the bushes. It is said that Dieskau's Iroquois, seeing Mohawks, their relatives, in the van, wished to warn them of danger. If so, the warning came too late. The thickets on the left blazed out a deadly fire, and the men fell by scores. In the words of Dieskau, the head of the column "was doubled up like a pack of cards." Hendrick's horse was shot down, and the chief was killed with a bayonet as he tried to rise. Williams, seeing a rising ground on his right, made for it, calling on his men to follow; but as he climbed the slope, guns flashed from the bushes, and a shot through the brain laid him dead. The men in the rear pressed forward to support their comrades, when a hot fire was suddenly opened on them from the forest along their right flank. Then there was a panic: some fled outright, and the whole column recoiled. The van now became the rear, and all the force of the enemy rushed upon it, shouting and screeching. There was a moment of total confusion; but a part of Williams's regiment rallied under command

of Whiting, and covered the retreat, fighting behind trees
like Indians, and firing and falling back by turns, bravely
aided by some of the Mohawks and by a detachment
which Johnson sent to their aid. "And a very hand-
some retreat they made," writes Pomeroy; "and so
continued till they came within about three quarters of
a mile of our camp. This was the last fire our men gave
our enemies, which killed great numbers of them; they
were seen to drop as pigeons." So ended the fray long
known in New England fireside story as the "bloody
morning scout." Dieskau now ordered a halt, and
sounded his trumpets to collect his scattered men. His
Indians, however, were sullen and unmanageable, and
the Canadians also showed signs of wavering. The
veteran who commanded them all, Legardeur de Saint-
Pierre, had been killed. At length they were persuaded
to move again, the regulars leading the way.

About an hour after Williams and his men had begun
their march, a distant rattle of musketry was heard at
the camp; and as it grew nearer and louder, the lis-
teners knew that their comrades were on the retreat.
Then, at the eleventh hour, preparations were begun for
defence. A sort of barricade was made along the front
of the camp, partly of wagons, and partly of inverted
bateaux, but chiefly of the trunks of trees hastily hewn
down in the neighboring forest and laid end to end in
a single row. The line extended from the southern
slopes of the hill on the left across a tract of rough
ground to the marshes on the right. The forest, choked
with bushes and clumps of rank ferns, was within a few
yards of the barricade, and there was scarcely time to
hack away the intervening thickets. Three cannon were
planted to sweep the road that descended through the
pines, and another was dragged up to the ridge of the

hill. The defeated party began to come in; first, scared
fugitives both white and red; then, gangs of men bringing the wounded; and at last, an hour and a half after
the first fire was heard, the main detachment was seen
marching in compact bodies down the road.

Five hundred men were detailed to guard the flanks
of the camp. The rest stood behind the wagons or lay
flat behind the logs and inverted bateaux, the Massachusetts men on the right, and the Connecticut men on the
left. Besides Indians, this actual fighting force was
between sixteen and seventeen hundred rustics, very few
of whom had been under fire before that morning. They
were hardly at their posts when they saw ranks of white-
coated soldiers moving down the road, and bayonets
that to them seemed innumerable glittering between the
boughs. At the same time a terrific burst of war-whoops
rose along the front; and, in the words of Pomeroy,
"the Canadians and Indians, helter-skelter, the woods
full of them, came running with undaunted courage right
down the hill upon us, expecting to make us flee."
Some of the men grew uneasy; while the chief officers,
sword in hand, threatened instant death to any who
should stir from their posts. If Dieskau had made an
assault at that instant, there could be little doubt of the
result.

This he well knew; but he was powerless. He had
his small force of regulars well in hand: but the rest,
red and white, were beyond control, scattering through
the woods and swamps, shouting, yelling, and firing from
behind trees. The regulars advanced with intrepidity towards the camp where the trees were thin, deployed, and
fired by platoons, till Captain Eyre, who commanded the
artillery, opened on them with grape, broke their ranks,
and compelled them to take to cover. The fusillade

was now general on both sides, and soon grew furious.
"Perhaps," Seth Pomeroy wrote to his wife, two days
after, "the hailstones from heaven were never much
thicker than their bullets came; but, blessed be God!
that did not in the least daunt or disturb us." Johnson
received a flesh-wound in the thigh, and spent the rest
of the day in his tent. Lyman took command; and it
is a marvel that he escaped alive, for he was four hours
in the heat of the fire, directing and animating the men.
"It was the most awful day my eyes ever beheld," wrote
Surgeon Williams to his wife; "there seemed to be
nothing but thunder and lightning and perpetual pillars
of smoke." To him, his colleague Doctor Pynchon, one
assistant, and a young student called "Billy," fell the
charge of the wounded of his regiment. "The bullets
flew about our ears all the time of dressing them; so
we thought best to leave our tent and retire a few rods
behind the shelter of a log-house." On the adjacent hill
stood one Blodget, who seems to have been a sutler,
watching, as well as bushes, trees, and smoke would let
him, the progress of the fight, of which he soon after
made and published a curious bird's-eye view. As the
wounded men were carried to the rear, the wagoners
about the camp took their guns and powder-horns, and
joined in the fray. A Mohawk, seeing one of these men
still unarmed, leaped over the barricade, tomahawked
the nearest Canadian, snatched his gun, and darted back
unhurt. The brave savage found no imitators among
his tribesmen, most of whom did nothing but utter a few
war-whoops, saying that they had come to see their
English brothers fight. Some of the French Indians
opened a distant flank fire from the high ground beyond
the swamp on the right, but were driven off by a few
shells dropped among them.

Dieskau had directed his first attack against the left and centre of Johnson's position. Making no impression here, he tried to force the right, where lay the regiments of Titcomb, Ruggles, and Williams. The fire was hot for about an hour. Titcomb was shot dead, a rod in front of the barricade, firing from behind a tree like a common soldier. At length Dieskau, exposing himself within short range of the English line, was hit in the leg. His adjutant, Montreuil, himself wounded, came to his aid, and was washing the injured limb with brandy, when the unfortunate commander was again hit in the knee and thigh. He seated himself behind a tree, while the Adjutant called two Canadians to carry him to the rear. One of them was instantly shot down. Montreuil took his place ; but Dieskau refused to be moved, bitterly denounced the Canadians and Indians, and ordered the Adjutant to leave him and lead the regulars in a last effort against the camp.

It was too late. Johnson's men, singly or in small squads, were already crossing their row of logs ; and in a few moments the whole dashed forward with a shout, falling upon the enemy with hatchets and the butts of their guns. The French and their allies fled. The wounded General still sat helpless by the tree, when he saw a soldier aiming at him. He signed to the man not to fire ; but he pulled trigger, shot him across the hips, leaped upon him, and ordered him in French to surrender. "I said," writes Dieskau, "'You rascal, why did you fire? You see a man lying in his blood on the ground, and you shoot him!' He answered : 'How did I know that you had not got a pistol? I had rather kill the devil than have the devil kill me.' 'You are a Frenchman?' I asked. 'Yes,' he replied ; 'it is more than ten years since I left Canada ;' whereupon several

others fell on me and stripped me. I told them to carry
me to their general, which they did. On learning who I
was, he sent for surgeons, and, though wounded himself,
refused all assistance till my wounds were dressed."

It was near five o'clock when the final rout took place.
Some time before, several hundred of the Canadians and
Indians had left the field and returned to the scene of
the morning fight, to plunder and scalp the dead. They
were resting themselves near a pool in the forest, close
beside the road, when their repose was interrupted by
a volley of bullets. It was fired by a scouting party
from Fort Lyman, chiefly backwoodsmen, under Captains
Folsom and McGinnis. The assailants were greatly
outnumbered; but after a hard fight the Canadians
and Indians broke and fled. McGinnis was mortally
wounded. He continued to give orders till the firing
was over; then fainted, and was carried, dying, to the
camp. The bodies of the slain, according to tradition,
were thrown into the pool, which bears to this day the
name of Bloody Pond.

The various bands of fugitives rejoined each other
towards night, and encamped in the forest; then made
their way round the southern shoulder of French Mountain, till, in the next evening, they reached their canoes.
Their plight was deplorable; for they had left their
knapsacks behind, and were spent with fatigue and
famine.

Meanwhile their captive general was not yet out of
danger. The Mohawks were furious at their losses in
the ambush of the morning, and above all at the death
of Hendrick. Scarcely were Dieskau's wounds dressed,
when several of them came into the tent. There was a
long and angry dispute in their own language between
them and Johnson, after which they went out very

sullenly. Dieskau asked what they wanted. "What do they want?" returned Johnson. "To burn you, by God, eat you, and smoke you in their pipes, in revenge for three or four of their chiefs that were killed. But never fear; you shall be safe with me, or else they shall kill us both." The Mohawks soon came back, and another talk ensued, excited at first, and then more calm; till at length the visitors, seemingly appeased, smiled, gave Dieskau their hands in sign of friendship, and quietly went out again. Johnson warned him that he was not yet safe; and when the prisoner, fearing that his presence might incommode his host, asked to be removed to another tent, a captain and fifty men were ordered to guard him. In the morning an Indian, alone and apparently unarmed, loitered about the entrance, and the stupid sentinel let him pass in. He immediately drew a sword from under a sort of cloak which he wore, and tried to stab Dieskau; but was prevented by the colonel to whom the tent belonged, who seized upon him, took away his sword, and pushed him out. As soon as his wounds would permit, Dieskau was carried on a litter, strongly escorted, to Fort Lyman, whence he was sent to Albany, and afterwards to New York. He is profuse in expressions of gratitude for the kindness shown him by the colonial officers, and especially by Johnson. Of the provincial soldiers he remarked soon after the battle that in the morning they fought like good boys, about noon like men, and in the afternoon like devils. In the spring of 1757 he sailed for England, and was for a time at Falmouth; whence Colonel Matthew Sewell, fearing that he might see and learn too much, wrote to the Earl of Holdernesse: "The Baron has great penetration and quickness of apprehension. His long service under Marshal Saxe renders him a man of real conse-

quence, to be cautiously observed. His circumstances
deserve compassion, for indeed they are very melancholy,
and I much doubt of his being ever perfectly cured."
He was afterwards a long time at Bath, for the benefit
of the waters. In 1760 the famous Diderot met him at
Paris, cheerful and full of anecdote, though wretchedly
shattered by his wounds. He died a few years later.

On the night after the battle the yeomen warriors felt
the truth of the saying that, next to defeat, the saddest
thing is victory. Comrades and friends by scores lay
scattered through the forest. As soon as he could snatch
a moment's leisure, the overworked surgeon sent the
dismal tidings to his wife : " My dear brother Ephraim
was killed by a ball through his head ; poor brother
Josiah's wound I fear will prove mortal ; poor Captain
Hawley is yet alive, though I did not think he would
live two hours after bringing him in." Daniel Pomeroy
was shot dead ; and his brother Seth wrote the news
to his wife Rachel, who was just delivered of a child :
" Dear Sister, this brings heavy tidings ; but let not
your heart sink at the news, though it be your loss of a
dear husband. Monday the eighth instant was a memorable day ; and truly you may say, had not the Lord
been on our side, we must all have been swallowed up.
My brother, being one that went out in the first engage-
ment, received a fatal shot through the middle of the
head." Seth Pomeroy found a moment to write also to
his own wife, whom he tells that another attack is expected ; adding, in quaintly pious phrase : " But as God
hath begun to show mercy, I hope he will go on to be
gracious." Pomeroy was employed during the next few
days with four hundred men in what he calls " the
melancholy piece of business" of burying the dead. A
letter-writer of the time does not approve what was done

on this occasion. " Our people," he says, " not only buried the French dead, but buried as many of them as might be without the knowledge of our Indians, to prevent their being scalped. This I call an excess of civility ; " his reason being that Braddock's dead soldiers had been left to the wolves.

The English loss in killed, wounded, and missing was two hundred and sixty-two ; and that of the French, by their own account, two hundred and twenty-eight, — a somewhat modest result of five hours' fighting. The English loss was chiefly in the ambush of the morning, where the killed greatly outnumbered the wounded, because those who fell and could not be carried away were tomahawked by Dieskau's Indians. In the fight at the camp, both Indians and Canadians kept themselves so well under cover that it was very difficult for the New England men to pick them off, while they on their part lay close behind their row of logs. On the French side, the regular officers and troops bore the brunt of the battle and suffered the chief loss, nearly all of the former and nearly half of the latter being killed or wounded.

Johnson did not follow up his success. He says that his men were tired. Yet five hundred of them had stood still all day, and boats enough for their transportation were lying on the beach. Ten miles down the lake, a path led over a gorge of the mountains to South Bay, where Dieskau had left his canoes and provisions. It needed but a few hours to reach and destroy them ; but no such attempt was made. Nor, till a week after, did Johnson send out scouts to learn the strength of the enemy at Ticonderoga. Lyman strongly urged him to make an effort to seize that important pass ; but Johnson thought only of holding his own position. " I think," he wrote, " we may expect very shortly a more formidable attack." He made a solid breastwork to defend his camp; and as reinforcements arrived, set them at building a fort, which he named Fort William Henry, on a rising ground by the lake. It is true that just after the battle he was deficient in stores, and had not bateaux enough to move his whole force. It is true, also, that he was wounded, and that he was too jealous of Lyman to delegate the command to him; and so the days passed till, within a fortnight, his nimble enemy were intrenched at Ticonderoga in force enough to defy him.

The Crown Point expedition was a failure disguised under an incidental success.

A WINTER RAID.

WHILE Johnson was building Fort William Henry at one end of Lake George, the French began Fort Ticonderoga at the other, though they did not finish it till the next year. In the winter of 1757, hearing that the English were making great preparations at Fort William Henry to attack them, they resolved to anticipate the blow and seize that post by surprise. To this end, Vaudreuil, Governor of Canada, sent a large detachment from Montreal, while the small body of troops and provincials who occupied the English fort remained wholly ignorant of the movement.

On St. Patrick's Day, the seventeenth of March, the Irish soldiers who formed a part of the garrison of Fort William Henry were paying homage to their patron saint in libations of heretic rum, the product of New England stills; and it is said that John Stark's rangers forgot theological differences in their zeal to share the festivity. The story adds that they were restrained by their commander, and that their enforced sobriety proved the saving of the fort. This may be doubted; for without counting the English soldiers of the garrison who had no special call to be drunk that day, the fort was in no danger till twenty-four hours after, when the revellers had had time to rally from their pious carouse. Whether rangers or British soldiers, it is certain that watchmen were on the alert during the night between the eighteenth and nineteenth, and that towards one in the morning they heard a sound of axes far down the lake, followed by the faint glow of a distant fire. The inference was plain, that an enemy was there, and that the necessity of warming himself had overcome his caution. Then all was still for some two hours, when, listening in the pitchy darkness, the watchers heard the footsteps of a great body of men approaching on the ice, which at the time was bare of snow. The garrison were at their posts, and all the cannon on the side towards the lake vomited grape and round-shot in the direction of the sound, which thereafter was heard no more.

Those who made it were the detachment, called by Vaudreuil an army, sent by him to seize the English fort. Shirley had planned a similar stroke against Ticonderoga a year before; but the provincial levies had come in so slowly, and the ice had broken up so soon, that the scheme was abandoned. Vaudreuil was more fortunate. The whole force, regulars, Canadians, and Indians, was ready to his hand. No pains were spared in equipping them. Overcoats, blankets, bearskins to sleep on, tarpaulins to sleep under, spare moccasons, spare mittens, kettles, axes, needles, awls, flint and steel, and many miscellaneous articles were provided, to be dragged by the men on light Indian sledges, along with provisions for twelve days. The cost of the expedition is set at a million francs, answering to more than as many dollars of the present time. To the disgust of the officers from France, the Governor named his brother Rigaud for the chief command; and before the end of February the whole party was on its march along the ice of Lake Champlain. They rested nearly a week at Ticonderoga, where no less than three hundred short scaling-ladders, so constructed that two or

more could be joined in one, had been made for them;
and here, too, they received a reinforcement, which
raised their number to sixteen hundred. Then, marching three days along Lake George, they neared the fort
on the evening of the eighteenth, and prepared for a
general assault before daybreak.

The garrison, including rangers, consisted of three
hundred and forty-six effective men. The fort was not
strong, and a resolute assault by numbers so superior
must, it seems, have overpowered the defenders; but
the Canadians and Indians who composed most of the
attacking force were not suited for such work; and,
disappointed in his hope of a surprise, Rigaud withdrew
them at daybreak, after trying in vain to burn the
buildings outside. A few hours after, the whole body
reappeared, filing off to surround the fort, on which they
kept up a brisk but harmless fire of musketry. In the
night they were heard again on the ice, approaching as
if for an assault; and the cannon, firing towards the
sound, again drove them back. There was silence for
a while, till tongues of flame lighted up the gloom, and
two sloops, ice-bound in the lake, and a large number of
bateaux on the shore were seen to be on fire. A party
sallied to save them; but it was too late. In the
morning they were all consumed, and the enemy had
vanished.

It was Sunday, the twentieth. Everything was quiet
till noon, when the French filed out of the woods and
marched across the ice in procession, ostentatiously
carrying their scaling-ladders, and showing themselves
to the best effect. They stopped at a safe distance,
fronting towards the fort, and several of them advanced,
waving a red flag. An officer with a few men went to
meet them, and returned bringing Le Mercier, chief of

the Canadian artillery, who, being led blindfold into the fort, announced himself as bearer of a message from Rigaud. He was conducted to the room of Major Eyre, where all the British officers were assembled; and, after mutual compliments, he invited them to give up the place peaceably, promising the most favorable terms, and threatening a general assault and massacre in case of refusal. Eyre said that he should defend himself to the last; and the envoy, again blindfolded, was led back to whence he came.

The whole French force now advanced as if to storm the works, and the garrison prepared to receive them. Nothing came of it but a fusillade, to which the British made no reply. At night the French were heard advancing again, and each man nerved himself for the crisis. The real attack, however, was not against the fort, but against the buildings outside, which consisted of several storehouses, a hospital, a saw-mill, and the huts of the rangers, besides a sloop on the stocks and piles of planks and cord-wood. Covered by the night, the assailants crept up with fagots of resinous sticks, placed them against the farther side of the buildings, kindled them, and escaped before the flame rose; while the garrison, straining their ears in the thick darkness, fired wherever they heard a sound. Before morning all around them was in a blaze, and they had much ado to save the fort barracks from the shower of burning cinders. At ten o'clock the fires had subsided, and a thick fall of snow began, filling the air with a restless chaos of large moist flakes. This lasted all day and all the next night, till the ground and the ice were covered to a depth of three feet and more. The French lay close in their camps till a little before dawn on Tuesday morning, when twenty volunteers from the regulars made a bold attempt to burn the sloop on the stocks, with several storehouses and other structures, and several hundred scows and whaleboats which had thus far escaped. They were only in part successful; but they fired the sloop and some buildings near it, and stood far out on the ice watching the flaming vessel, a superb bonfire amid the wilderness of snow. The spectacle cost the volunteers a fourth of their number killed and wounded.

On Wednesday morning the sun rose bright on a scene of wintry splendor, and the frozen lake was dotted with Rigaud's retreating followers toiling towards Canada on snow-shoes. Before they reached it many of them were blinded for a while by the insufferable glare, and their comrades led them homewards by the hand.

SIEGE AND MASSACRE OF FORT WILLIAM HENRY.

HAVING failed to take Fort William Henry by surprise, the French resolved to attack it with all the force they could bring against it, and in the summer of 1757 the Marquis de Montcalm and the Chevalier de Lévis advanced against it with about eight thousand regulars, Canadians, and Indians. The whole assembled at Ticonderoga, where several weeks were spent in preparation. Provisions, camp equipage, ammunition, cannon, and bateaux were dragged by gangs of men up the road to the head of the rapids. The work went on through heat and rain, by day and night, till, at the end of July, all was done.

The bateaux lay ready by the shore, but could not carry the whole force; and Lévis received orders to march by the side of the lake with twenty-five hundred men, Canadians, regulars, and Iroquois. He set out at daybreak of the thirtieth of July, his men carrying nothing but their knapsacks, blankets, and weapons. Guided by the unerring Indians, they climbed the steep gorge at the side of Rogers Rock, gained the valley beyond, and marched southward along a Mohawk trail which threaded the forest in a course parallel to the lake. The way was of the roughest; many straggled from the line, and two officers completely broke down. The first destination of the party was the mouth of Ganouskie Bay,

now called Northwest Bay, where they were to wait for
Montcalm, and kindle three fires as a signal that they
had reached the rendezvous.

Montcalm left a detachment to hold Ticonderoga;
and then, on the first of August, at two in the afternoon,
he embarked at the Burned Camp with all his remaining
force. Including those with Lévis, the expedition counted
about seven thousand six hundred men, of whom more
than sixteen hundred were Indians. At five in the
afternoon they reached the place where the Indians, who
had gone on before the rest, were smoking their pipes
and waiting for the army. The red warriors embarked,
and joined the French flotilla; and now, as evening drew
near, was seen one of those wild pageantries of war
which Lake George has often witnessed. A restless
multitude of birch canoes, filled with painted savages,
glided by shores and islands, like troops of swimming
water-fowl. Two hundred and fifty bateaux came next,
moved by sail and oar, some bearing the Canadian
militia, and some the battalions of Old France in trim
and gay attire: first, La Reine and Languedoc; then
the colony regulars; then La Sarre and Guienne; then
the Canadian brigade of Courtemanche; then the cannon and mortars, each on a platform sustained by two
bateaux lashed side by side, and rowed by the militia of
Saint-Ours; then the battalions of Béarn and Royal
Roussillon; then the Canadians of Gaspé, with the pro-
vision-bateaux and the field-hospital; and, lastly, a rear
guard of regulars closed the line. So, under the flush
of sunset, they held their course along the romantic
lake, to play their part in the historic drama that lends
a stern enchantment to its fascinating scenery. They
passed the Narrows in mist and darkness; and when, a
little before dawn, they rounded the high promontory of

Tongue Mountain, they saw, far on the right, three fiery sparks shining through the gloom. These were the signal-fires of Lévis, to tell them that he had reached the appointed spot.

Lévis had arrived the evening before, after his hard march through the sultry midsummer forest. His men had now rested for a night, and at ten in the morning he marched again. Montcalm followed at noon, and coasted the western shore, till, towards evening, he found Lévis waiting for him by the margin of a small bay not far from the English fort, though hidden from it by a projecting point of land. Canoes and bateaux were drawn up on the beach, and the united forces made their bivouac together.

The earthen mounds of Fort William Henry still stand by the brink of Lake George; and seated at the sunset of an August day under the pines that cover them, one gazes on a scene of soft and soothing beauty, where dreamy waters reflect the glories of the mountains and the sky. As it is to-day, so it was then; all breathed repose and peace. The splash of some leaping trout, or the dipping wing of a passing swallow, alone disturbed the summer calm of that unruffled mirror.

About ten o'clock at night two boats set out from the fort to reconnoitre. They were passing a point of land on their left, two miles or more down the lake, when the men on board descried through the gloom a strange object against the bank; and they rowed towards it to learn what it might be. It was an awning over the bateau that carried Roubaud and his brother missionaries. As the rash oarsmen drew near, the bleating of a sheep in one of the French provision-boats warned them of danger; and turning, they pulled for their lives towards the eastern shore. Instantly more than a thousand

Indians threw themselves into their canoes and dashed in hot pursuit, making the lake and the mountains ring with the din of their war-whoops. The fugitives had nearly reached land when their pursuers opened fire. They replied; shot one Indian dead, and wounded another; then snatched their oars again, and gained the beach. But the whole savage crew was upon them. Several were killed, three were taken, and the rest escaped in the dark woods. The prisoners were brought before Montcalm, and gave him valuable information of the strength and position of the English.[1]

The Indian who was killed was a noted chief of the Nipissings; and his tribesmen howled in grief for their bereavement. They painted his face with vermilion, tied feathers in his hair, hung pendants in his ears and nose, clad him in a resplendent war-dress, put silver bracelets on his arms, hung a gorget on his breast with a flame-colored ribbon, and seated him in state on the top of a hillock, with his lance in his hand, his gun in the hollow of his arm, his tomahawk in his belt, and his kettle by his side. Then they all crouched about him in lugubrious silence. A funeral harangue followed; and next a song and solemn dance to the thumping of the Indian drum. In the gray of the morning they buried him as he sat, and placed food in the grave for his journey to the land of souls.

As the sun rose above the eastern mountains the French camp was all astir. The column of Lévis, with Indians to lead the way, moved through the forest towards the fort, and Montcalm followed with the main

---

[1] The remains of Fort William Henry are now crowded between a hotel and the wharf and station of a railway. A scheme has been set on foot to level the whole for other railway structures. When I first knew the place the ground was in much the same state as in the time of Montcalm.

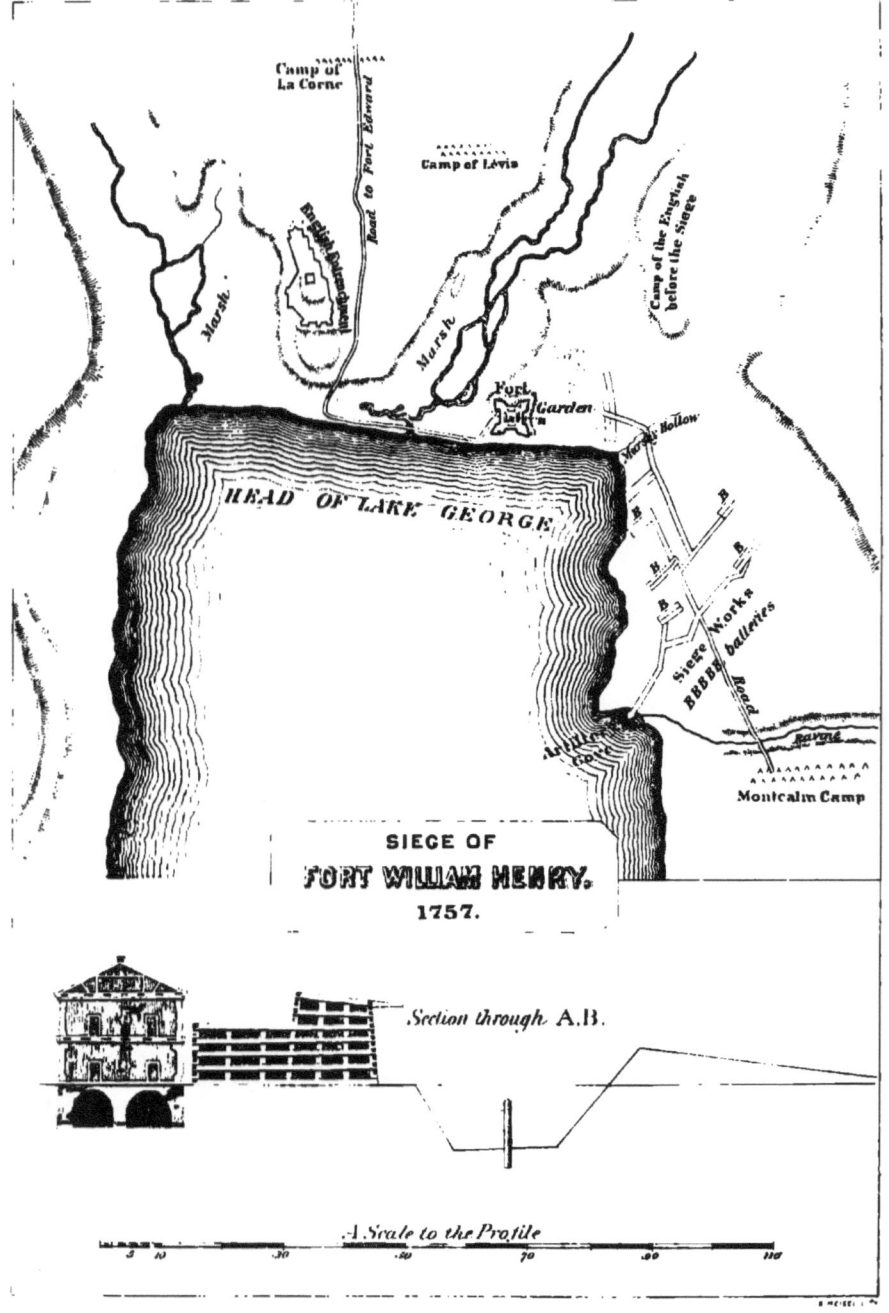

SIEGE OF

FORT WILLIAM HENRY.

1757.

Section through A.B.

A Scale to the Profile

body; then the artillery boats rounded the point that had hid them from the sight of the English, saluting them as they did so with musketry and cannon; while a host of savages put out upon the lake, ranged their canoes abreast in a line from shore to shore, and advanced slowly, with measured paddle-strokes and yells of defiance.

The position of the enemy was full in sight before them. At the head of the lake, towards the right, stood the fort, close to the edge of the water. On its left was a marsh; then the rough piece of ground where Johnson had encamped two years before; then a low, flat, rocky hill, crowned with an intrenched camp; and, lastly, on the extreme left, another marsh. Far around the fort and up the slopes of the western mountain the forest had been cut down and burned, and the ground was cumbered with blackened stumps and charred carcasses and limbs of fallen trees, strewn in savage disorder one upon another. Distant shouts and war-cries, the clatter of musketry, white puffs of smoke in the dismal clearing and along the scorched edge of the bordering forest, told that Lévis' Indians were skirmishing with parties of the English, who had gone out to save the cattle roaming in the neighborhood, and burn some out-buildings that would have favored the besiegers. Others were taking down the tents that stood on a plateau near the foot of the mountain on the right, and moving them to the intrenchment on the hill. The garrison sallied from the fort to support their comrades, and for a time the firing was hot.

Fort William Henry was an irregular bastioned square, formed by embankments of gravel surmounted by a rampart of heavy logs, laid in tiers crossed one upon another, the interstices filled with earth. The lake pro-

4

tected it on the north, the marsh on the east, and ditches with *chevaux-de-frise* on the south and west. Seventeen cannon, great and small, besides several mortars and swivels, were mounted upon it; and a brave Scotch veteran, Lieutenant-Colonel Monro, of the thirty-fifth regiment, was in command.

General Webb lay fourteen miles distant at Fort Edward, with twenty-six hundred men, chiefly provincials. On the twenty-fifth of July he had made a visit to Fort William Henry, examined the place, given some orders, and returned on the twenty-ninth. He then wrote to the Governor of New York, telling him that the French were certainly coming, begging him to send up the militia, and saying: " I am determined to march to Fort William Henry with the whole army under my command as soon as I shall hear of the farther approach of the enemy." Instead of doing so he waited three days, and then sent up a detachment of two hundred regulars under Lieutenant-Colonel Young, and eight hundred Massachusetts men under Colonel Frye. This raised the force at the lake to two thousand and two hundred, including sailors and mechanics, and reduced that of Webb to sixteen hundred, besides half as many more distributed at Albany and the intervening forts. If, according to his spirited intention, he should go to the rescue of Monro, he must leave some of his troops behind him to protect the lower posts from a possible French inroad by way of South Bay. Thus his power of aiding Monro was slight, so rashly had Loudon, intent on Louisbourg, left this frontier open to attack. The defect, however, was as much in Webb himself as in his resources. His conduct in the past year had raised doubts of his personal courage; and this was the moment for answering them. Great as was the disparity of numbers,

the emergency would have justified an attempt to save
Monro at any risk.   That officer sent him a hasty note,
written at nine o'clock on the morning of the third,
telling him that the French were in sight on the lake;
and, in the next night, three rangers came to Fort
Edward, bringing another short note, dated at six in the
evening, announcing that the firing had begun, and clos-
ing with the words: "I believe you will think it proper
to send a reinforcement as soon as possible."   Now, if
ever, was the time to move, before the fort was invested
and access cut off.   But Webb lay quiet, sending expresses to New England for help which could not possibly
arrive in time.   On the next night another note came
from Monro to say that the French were upon him in
great numbers, well supplied with artillery, but that the
garrison were all in good spirits.   "I make no doubt,"
wrote the hard-pressed officer, "that you will soon send
us a reinforcement;" and again on the same day: "We
are very certain that a part of the enemy have got between you and us upon the high road, and would therefore be glad (if it meets with your approbation) the
whole army was marched."   But Webb gave no sign.

When the skirmishing around the fort was over, La
Corne, with a body of Indians, occupied the road that
led to Fort Edward, and Lévis encamped hard by to
support him, while Montcalm proceeded to examine the
ground and settle his plan of attack.   He made his way
to the rear of the intrenched camp and reconnoitred it,
hoping to carry it by assault; but it had a breastwork
of stones and logs, and he thought the attempt too haz-
ardous.   The ground where he stood was that where
Dieskau had been defeated; and as the fate of his pre-
decessor was not of flattering augury, he resolved to
besiege the fort in form.

He chose for the site of his operations the ground now covered by the village of Caldwell. A little to the north of it was a ravine, beyond which he formed his main camp, while Lévis occupied a tract of dry ground beside the marsh, whence he could easily move to intercept succors from Fort Edward on the one hand, or repel a sortie from Fort William Henry on the other. A brook ran down the ravine and entered the lake at a small cove protected from the fire of the fort by a point of land; and at this place, still called Artillery Cove, Montcalm prepared to debark his cannon and mortars.

Having made his preparations, he sent Fontbrune, one of his aides-de-camp, with a letter to Monro. "I owe it to humanity," he wrote, "to summon you to surrender. At present I can restrain the savages, and make them observe the terms of a capitulation, as I might not have power to do under other circumstances; and an obstinate defence on your part could only retard the capture of the place a few days, and endanger an unfortunate garrison which cannot be relieved, in consequence of the dispositions I have made. I demand a decisive answer within an hour." Monro replied that he and his soldiers would defend themselves to the last. While the flags of truce were flying, the Indians swarmed over the fields before the fort; and when they learned the result, an Abenaki chief shouted in broken French: "You won't surrender, eh! Fire away then, and fight your best; for if I catch you, you shall get no quarter." Monro emphasized his refusal by a general discharge of his cannon.

The trenches were opened on the night of the fourth, —a task of extreme difficulty, as the ground was covered by a profusion of half-burned stumps, roots, branches, and fallen trunks. Eight hundred men toiled till daylight with pick, spade, and axe, while the cannon from

the fort flashed through the darkness, and grape and
round-shot whistled and screamed over their heads.
Some of the English balls reached the camp beyond the
ravine, and disturbed the slumbers of the officers off
duty, as they lay wrapped in their blankets and bearskins. Before daybreak the first parallel was made; a
battery was nearly finished on the left, and another was
begun on the right. The men now worked under cover,
safe in their burrows; one gang relieved another, and
the work went on all day.

The Indians were far from doing what was expected
of them. Instead of scouting in the direction of Fort
Edward to learn the movements of the enemy and prevent surprise, they loitered about the camp and in the
trenches, or amused themselves by firing at the fort
from behind stumps and logs. Some, in imitation of
the French, dug little trenches for themselves, in which
they wormed their way towards the rampart, and now
and then picked off an artillery-man, not without loss on
their own side. On the afternoon of the fifth, Montcalm
invited them to a council, gave them belts of wampum,
and mildly remonstrated with them. " Why expose
yourselves without necessity ? I grieve bitterly over the
losses that you have met, for the least among you is
precious to me. No doubt it is a good thing to annoy
the English ; but that is not the main point. You ought
to inform me of everything the enemy is doing, and
always keep parties on the road between the two forts."
And he gently hinted that their place was not in his
camp, but in that of Lévis, where missionaries were
provided for such of them as were Christians, and food
and ammunition for them all. They promised, with
excellent docility, to do everything he wished, but
added that there was something on their hearts. Being

encouraged to relieve themselves of the burden, they complained that they had not been consulted as to the management of the siege, but were expected to obey orders like slaves. " We know more about fighting in the woods than you," said their orator; "ask our advice, and you will be the better for it."

Montcalm assured them that if they had been neglected, it was only through the hurry and confusion of the time : expressed high appreciation of their talents for bush-fighting, promised them ample satisfaction, and ended by telling them that in the morning they should hear the big guns. This greatly pleased them, for they were extremely impatient for the artillery to begin. About sunrise the battery of the left opened with eight heavy cannon and a mortar, joined, on the next morning, by the battery of the right, with eleven pieces more. The fort replied with spirit. The cannon thundered all day, and from a hundred peaks and crags the astonished wilderness roared back the sound. The Indians were delighted. They wanted to point the guns; and to humor them, they were now and then allowed to do so. Others lay behind logs and fallen trees, and yelled their satisfaction when they saw the splinters fly from the wooden rampart.

Day after day the weary roar of the distant cannonade fell on the ears of Webb in his camp at Fort Edward. " I have not yet received the least reinforcement," he writes to Loudon ; " this is the disagreeable situation we are at present in. The fort, by the heavy firing we hear from the lake, is still in our possession ; but I fear it cannot long hold out against so warm a cannonading if I am not reinforced by a sufficient number of militia to march to their relief." The militia were coming ; but it was impossible that many could reach him in less

than a week. Those from New York alone were within
call, and two thousand of them arrived soon after he
sent Loudon the above letter. Then, by stripping all
the forts below, he could bring together forty-five hundred men; while several French deserters assured him
that Montcalm had nearly twelve thousand. To advance
to the relief of Monro with a force so inferior, through
a defile of rocks, forests, and mountains, made by nature
for ambuscades, — and this too with troops who had
neither the steadiness of regulars nor the bush-fighting
skill of Indians, — was an enterprise for firmer nerve
than his.

He had already warned Monro to expect no help from
him. At midnight of the fourth, Captain Bartman, his
aide-de-camp, wrote: "The General has ordered me to
acquaint you he does not think it prudent to attempt a
junction or to assist you till reinforced by the militia
of the colonies, for the immediate march of which repeated expresses have been sent." The letter then
declared that the French were in complete possession
of the road between the two forts, that a prisoner just
brought in reported their force in men and cannon to
be very great, and that, unless the militia came soon,
Monro had better make what terms he could with the
enemy.

The chance was small that this letter would reach its
destination; and in fact the bearer was killed by La
Corne's Indians, who, in stripping the body, found the
hidden paper, and carried it to the General. Montcalm
kept it several days, till the English rampart was half
battered down; and then, after saluting his enemy with
a volley from all his cannon, he sent it with a graceful
compliment to Monro. It was Bougainville who carried
it, preceded by a drummer and a flag. He was met at

the foot of the glacis, blindfolded, and led through the
fort and along the edge of the lake to the intrenched
camp, where Monro was at the time. "He returned
many thanks," writes the emissary in his Diary, "for
the courtesy of our nation, and protested his joy at
having to do with so generous an enemy. This was
his answer to the Marquis de Montcalm. Then they led
me back, always with eyes blinded; and our batteries
began to fire again as soon as we thought that the English grenadiers who escorted me had had time to re-enter
the fort. I hope General Webb's letter may induce the
English to surrender the sooner."

By this time the sappers had worked their way to the
angle of the lake, where they were stopped by a marshy
hollow, beyond which was a tract of high ground, reaching to the fort and serving as the garden of the garrison.[1]
Logs and fascines in large quantities were thrown into
the hollow, and hurdles were laid over them to form a
causeway for the cannon. Then the sap was continued
up the acclivity beyond, a trench was opened in the
garden, and a battery begun, not two hundred and fifty
yards from the fort. The Indians, in great number,
crawled forward among the beans, maize, and cabbages,
and lay there ensconced. On the night of the seventh,
two men came out of the fort. apparently to reconnoitre,
with a view to a sortie, when they were greeted by a
general volley and a burst of yells which echoed among
the mountains; followed by responsive whoops pealing
through the darkness from the various camps and lurk-
ing-places of the savage warriors far and near.

The position of the besieged was now deplorable.
More than three hundred of them had been killed and

---

[1] Now the site of Fort William Henry Hotel, with its grounds. The
hollow is partly filled by the main road of Caldwell.

wounded; small-pox was raging in the fort; the place
was a focus of infection, and the casemates were crowded
with the sick. A sortie from the intrenched camp and
another from the fort had been repulsed with loss. All
their large cannon and mortars had been burst, or disabled by shot; only seven small pieces were left fit for
service; and the whole of Montcalm's thirty-one cannon
and fifteen mortars and howitzers would soon open fire,
while the walls were already breached, and an assault
was imminent. Through the night of the eighth they
fired briskly from all their remaining pieces. In the
morning the officers held a council, and all agreed to
surrender if honorable terms could be had. A white
flag was raised, a drum was beat, and Lieutenant-Colonel
Young, mounted on horseback, — for a shot in the foot
had disabled him from walking, — went, followed by a
few soldiers, to the tent of Montcalm.

It was agreed that the English troops should march
out with the honors of war, and be escorted to Fort
Edward by a detachment of French troops; that they
should not serve for eighteen months; and that all
French prisoners captured in America since the war
began should be given up within three months. The
stores, munitions, and artillery were to be the prize of
the victors, except one field-piece, which the garrison
were to retain in recognition of their brave defence.

Before signing the capitulation Montcalm called the
Indian chiefs to council, and asked them to consent to
the conditions, and promise to restrain their young
warriors from any disorder. They approved everything
and promised everything. The garrison then evacuated
the fort, and marched to join their comrades in the
intrenched camp, which was included in the surrender. No sooner were they gone than a crowd of Indians

clambered through the embrasures in search of rum and plunder. All the sick men unable to leave their beds were instantly butchered. "I was witness of this spectacle," says the missionary Roubaud; "I saw one of these barbarians come out of the casemates with a human head in his hand, from which the blood ran in streams, and which he paraded as if he had got the finest prize in the world." There was little left to plunder; and the Indians, joined by the more lawless of the Canadians, turned their attention to the intrenched camp, where all the English were now collected.

The French guard stationed there could not or would not keep out the rabble. By the advice of Montcalm the English stove their rum-barrels; but the Indians were drunk already with homicidal rage, and the glitter of their vicious eyes told of the devil within. They roamed among the tents, intrusive, insolent, their visages besmirched with war-paint; grinning like fiends as they handled, in anticipation of the knife, the long hair of cowering women, of whom, as well as of children, there were many in the camp, all crazed with fright. Since the last war the New England border population had regarded Indians with a mixture of detestation and horror. Their mysterious warfare of ambush and surprise, their midnight onslaughts, their butcheries, their burnings, and all their nameless atrocities, had been for years the theme of fireside story; and the dread they excited was deepened by the distrust and dejection of the time. The confusion in the camp lasted through the afternoon. "The Indians," says Bougainville, "wanted to plunder the chests of the English; the latter resisted; and there was fear that serious disorder would ensue. The Marquis de Montcalm ran thither immediately, and used every means to restore tranquillity: prayers,

threats, caresses, interposition of the officers and interpreters who have some influence over these savages."
" We shall be but too happy if we can prevent a massacre. Detestable position! of which nobody who has
not been in it can have any idea, and which makes
victory itself a sorrow to the victors. The Marquis
spared no efforts to prevent the rapacity of the savages
and, I must say it, of certain persons associated with
them, from resulting in something worse than plunder.
At last, at nine o'clock in the evening, order seemed
restored. The Marquis even induced the Indians to
promise that, besides the escort agreed upon in the
capitulation, two chiefs for each tribe should accom-
pany the English on their way to Fort Edward." He
also ordered La Corne and the other Canadian officers
attached to the Indians to see that no violence took
place. He might well have done more. In view of the
disorders of the afternoon, it would not have been too
much if he had ordered the whole body of regular troops,
whom alone he could trust for the purpose, to hold
themselves ready to move to the spot in case of out-
break, and shelter their defeated foes behind a hedge of
bayonets.

Bougainville was not to see what ensued; for Montcalm
now sent him to Montreal, as a special messenger to
carry news of the victory. He embarked at ten o'clock.
Returning daylight found him far down the lake; and
as he looked on its still bosom flecked with mists, and
its quiet mountains sleeping under the flush of dawn,
there was nothing in the wild tranquillity of the scene
to suggest the tragedy which even then was beginning
on the shore he had left behind.

The English in their camp had passed a troubled
night, agitated by strange rumors. In the morning

something like a panic seized them; for they distrusted
not the Indians only, but the Canadians.   In their
haste to be gone they got together at daybreak, before the escort of three hundred regulars had arrived.
They had their muskets, but no ammunition; and few
or none of the provincials had bayonets.   Early as it
was, the Indians were on the alert; and, indeed, since
midnight great numbers of them had been prowling
about the skirts of the camp, showing, says Colonel
Frye, " more than usual malice in their looks."   Seventeen wounded men of his regiment lay in huts, unable
to join the march.   In the preceding afternoon Miles
Whitworth, the regimental surgeon, had passed them
over to the care of a French surgeon, according to an
agreement made at the time of the surrender; but, the
Frenchman being absent, the other remained with them
attending to their wants.   The French surgeon had
caused special sentinels to be posted for their protection.
These were now removed, at the moment when they
were needed most; upon which, about five o'clock in the
morning, the Indians entered the huts, dragged out the
inmates, and tomahawked and scalped them all, before
the eyes of Whitworth, and in presence of La Corne
and other Canadian officers, as well as of a French guard
stationed within forty feet of the spot; and, declares the
surgeon under oath, " none, either officer or soldier, protected the said wounded men."   The opportune butchery
relieved them of a troublesome burden.

A scene of plundering now began.   The escort had by
this time arrived, and Monro complained to the officers
that the capitulation was broken; but got no other answer than advice to give up the baggage to the Indians
in order to appease them.   To this the English at length
agreed; but it only increased the excitement of the mob.

They demanded rum; and some of the soldiers, afraid to refuse, gave it to them from their canteens, thus adding fuel to the flame. When, after much difficulty, the column at last got out of the camp and began to move along the road that crossed the rough plain between the intrenchment and the forest, the Indians crowded upon them, impeded their march, snatched caps, coats, and weapons from men and officers, tomahawked those that resisted, and seizing upon shrieking women and children, dragged them off or murdered them on the spot. It is said that some of the interpreters secretly fomented the disorder. Suddenly there rose the screech of the warwhoop. At this signal of butchery, which was given by Abenaki Christians from the mission of the Penobscot, a mob of savages rushed upon the New Hampshire men at the rear of the column, and killed or dragged away eighty of them. A frightful tumult ensued, when Montcalm, Lévis, Bourlamaque, and many other French officers, who had hastened from their camp on the first news of disturbance, threw themselves among the Indians, and by promises and threats tried to allay their frenzy. "Kill me, but spare the English who are under my protection," exclaimed Montcalm. He took from one of them a young officer whom the savage had seized; upon which several other Indians immediately tomahawked their prisoners, lest they too should be taken from them. One writer says that a French grenadier was killed and two wounded in attempting to restore order; but the statement is doubtful. The English seemed paralyzed, and fortunately did not attempt a resistance, which, without ammunition as they were, would have ended in a general massacre. Their broken column struggled forward in wild disorder, amid the din of whoops and shrieks, till they reached the French advance-guard, which consisted of Canadians;

and here they demanded protection from the officers,
who refused to give it, telling them that they must
take to the woods and shift for themselves. Frye was
seized by a number of Indians, who, brandishing spears
and tomahawks, threatened him with death and tore off
his clothing, leaving nothing but breeches, shoes, and
shirt. Repelled by the officers of the guard, he made
for the woods. A Connecticut soldier who was present
says of him that he leaped upon an Indian who stood in
his way, disarmed and killed him, and then escaped;
but Frye himself does not mention the incident. Captain Burke, also of the Massachusetts regiment, was
stripped, after a violent struggle, of all his clothes; then
broke loose, gained the woods, spent the night shivering
in the thick grass of a marsh, and on the next day
reached Fort Edward. Jonathan Carver, a provincial
volunteer, declares that, when the tumult was at its
height, he saw officers of the French army walking about
at a little distance and talking with seeming unconcern.
Three or four Indians seized him, brandished their tomahawks over his head, and tore off most of his clothes,
while he vainly claimed protection from a sentinel, who
called him an English dog, and violently pushed him
back among his tormentors. Two of them were drag-
ging him towards the neighboring swamp, when an
English officer, stripped of everything but his scarlet
breeches, ran by. One of Carver's captors sprang upon
him, but was thrown to the ground; whereupon the
other went to the aid of his comrade and drove his
tomahawk into the back of the Englishman. As Carver
turned to run, an English boy, about twelve years old,
clung to him and begged for help. They ran on together
for a moment, when the boy was seized, dragged from
his protector, and, as Carver judged by his shrieks, was

murdered. He himself escaped to the forest, and after three days of famine reached Fort Edward.

The bonds of discipline seem for the time to have been completely broken; for while Montcalm and his chief officers used every effort to restore order, even at the risk of their lives, many other officers, chiefly of the militia, failed atrociously to do their duty. How many English were killed it is impossible to tell with exactness. Roubaud says that he saw forty or fifty corpses scattered about the field. Lévis says fifty; which does not include the sick and wounded before murdered in the camp and fort. It is certain that six or seven hundred persons were carried off, stripped, and otherwise maltreated. Montcalm succeeded in recovering more than four hundred of them in the course of the day; and many of the French officers did what they could to relieve their wants by buying back from their captors the clothing that had been torn from them. Many of the fugitives had taken refuge in the fort, whither Monro himself had gone to demand protection for his followers; and here Roubaud presently found a crowd of half-frenzied women, crying in anguish for husbands and children. All the refugees and redeemed prisoners were afterwards conducted to the intrenched camp, where food and shelter were provided for them, and a strong guard set for their protection until the fifteenth, when they were sent under an escort to Fort Edward. Here cannon had been fired at intervals to guide those who had fled to the woods, whence they came dropping in from day to day, half dead with famine.

On the morning after the massacre the Indians decamped in a body and set out for Montreal, carrying with them their plunder and some two hundred prisoners, who, it is said, could not be got out of their hands.

The soldiers were set to the work of demolishing the English fort; and the task occupied several days. The barracks were torn down, and the huge pine-logs of the rampart thrown into a heap. The dead bodies that filled the casemates were added to the mass, and fire was set to the whole. The mighty funeral pyre blazed all night. Then, on the sixteenth, the army reimbarked. The din of ten thousand combatants, the rage, the terror, the agony, were gone; and no living thing was left but the wolves that gathered from the mountains to feast upon the dead.

MONTCALM.

AGED 29.

BATTLE OF TICONDEROGA.

IN 1758, the English commanders, incensed at the loss of Fort William Henry, resolved to retaliate by a strong effort to seize Ticonderoga. In June, the combined British and provincial force destined for the expedition was gathered at the head of Lake George under General Abercromby, while the Marquis de Montcalm lay around the walls of the French stronghold with an army not one fourth so numerous.

Montcalm hesitated whether he should not fall back to Crown Point. It was but a choice of difficulties, and he stayed at Ticonderoga. His troops were disposed as they had been in the summer before; one battalion, that of Berry, being left near the fort, while the main body, under Montcalm himself, was encamped by the saw-mill at the Falls, and the rest, under Bourlamaque, occupied the head of the portage, with a small advanced force at the landing-place on Lake George. It remained to determine at which of these points he should concentrate them and make his stand against the English. Ruin threatened him in any case; each position had its fatal weakness or its peculiar danger, and his best hope was in the ignorance or blundering of his enemy. He seems to have been several days in a state of indecision.

In the afternoon of the fifth of July the partisan Langy, who had gone out to reconnoitre towards the head of Lake George, came back in haste with the report that the English were embarked in great force. Montcalm sent a canoe down Lake Champlain to hasten Lévis to his aid, and ordered the battalion of Berry to begin a breastwork and abatis on the high ground in front of the fort. That they were not begun before shows that he was in doubt as to his plan of defence; and that his whole army was not now set to work at them shows that his doubt was still unsolved.

It was nearly a month since Abercromby had begun his camp at the head of Lake George. Here, on the ground where Johnson had beaten Dieskau, where Montcalm had planted his batteries, and Monro vainly defended the wooden ramparts of Fort William Henry, were now assembled more than fifteen thousand men; and the shores, the foot of the mountains, and the broken plains between them were studded thick with tents. Of regulars there were six thousand three hundred and sixty-seven, officers and soldiers, and of provincials nine thousand and thirty-four. To the New England levies, or at least to their chaplains, the expedition seemed a crusade against the abomination of Babylon; and they discoursed in their sermons of Moses sending forth Joshua against Amalek. Abercromby, raised to his place by political influence, was little but the nominal commander. "A heavy man," said Wolfe in a letter to his father; "an aged gentleman, infirm in body and mind," wrote William Parkman, a boy of seventeen, who carried a musket in a Massachusetts regiment, and kept in his knapsack a dingy little note-book, in which he jotted down what passed each day. The age of the aged gentleman was fifty-two.

Pitt meant that the actual command of the army should be in the hands of Brigadier Lord Howe, and he was in fact its real chief; "the noblest Englishman that has appeared in my time, and the best soldier in the British army," says Wolfe. And he elsewhere speaks of him as "that great man." Abercromby testifies to the universal respect and love with which officers and men regarded him, and Pitt calls him "a character of ancient times ; a complete model of military virtue." High as this praise is, it seems to have been deserved. The young nobleman, who was then in his thirty-fourth year, had the qualities of a leader of men. The army felt him, from general to drummer boy. He was its soul ; and while breathing into it his own energy and ardor, and bracing it by stringent discipline, he broke through the traditions of the service and gave it new shapes to suit the time and place. During the past year he had studied the art of forest warfare, and joined Rogers and his rangers in their scouting-parties, sharing all their hardships and making himself one of them. Perhaps the reforms that he introduced were fruits of this rough self-imposed schooling. He made officers and men throw off all useless incumbrances, cut their hair close, wear leggings to protect them from briers, brown the barrels of their muskets, and carry in their knapsacks thirty pounds of meal, which they cooked for themselves ; so that, according to an admiring Frenchman, they could live a month without their supply-trains. "You would laugh to see the droll figure we all make," writes an officer. "Regulars as well as provincials have cut their coats so as scarcely to reach their waists. No officer or private is allowed to carry more than one blanket and a bearskin. A small portmanteau is allowed each officer. No women follow the camp to wash our linen. Lord Howe has already shown an example by going to the brook and washing his own."

Here, as in all things, he shared the lot of the soldier,

and required his officers to share it. A story is told of him that before the army embarked he invited some of them to dinner in his tent, where they found no seats but logs, and no carpet but bearskins. A servant presently placed on the ground a large dish of pork and peas, on which his lordship took from his pocket a sheath containing a knife and fork and began to cut the meat. The guests looked on in some embarrassment; upon which he said: "Is it possible, gentlemen, that you have come on this campaign without providing yourselves with what is necessary?" And he gave each of them a sheath, with a knife and fork, like his own.

Yet this Lycurgus of the camp, as a contemporary calls him, is described as a man of social accomplishments rare even in his rank. He made himself greatly beloved by the provincial officers, with many of whom he was on terms of intimacy, and he did what he could to break down the barriers between the colonial soldiers and the British regulars. When he was at Albany, sharing with other high officers the kindly hospitalities of Mrs. Schuyler, he so won the heart of that excellent matron that she loved him like a son ; and, though not given to such effusion, embraced him with tears on the morning when he left her to lead his division to the lake. In Westminster Abbey may be seen the tablet on which Massachusetts pays grateful tribute to his virtues, and commemorates " the affection her officers and soldiers bore to his command."

On the evening of the fourth of July, baggage, stores, and ammunition were all on board the boats, and the whole army embarked on the morning of the fifth. The arrangements were perfect. Each corps marched without confusion to its appointed station on the beach, and the sun was scarcely above the ridge of French Moun-

tain when all were afloat. A spectator watching them
from the shore says that when the fleet was three miles
on its way, the surface of the lake at that distance was
completely hidden from sight. There were nine hundred bateaux, a hundred and thirty-five whaleboats, and
a large number of heavy flat boats carrying the artillery.
The whole advanced in three divisions, the regulars in
the centre, and the provincials on the flanks. Each
corps had its flags and its music. The day was fair, and
men and officers were in the highest spirits.

Before ten o'clock they began to enter the Narrows;
and the boats of the three divisions extended themselves
into long files as the mountains closed on either hand
upon the contracted lake. From front to rear the line
was six miles long. The spectacle was superb: the
brightness of the summer day; the romantic beauty of
the scenery; the sheen and sparkle of those crystal
waters; the countless islets, tufted with pine, birch, and
fir; the bordering mountains, with their green summits
and sunny crags; the flash of oars and glitter of weapons; the banners, the varied uniforms, and the notes of
bugle, trumpet, bagpipe, and drum, answered and pro-
longed by a hundred woodland echoes. "I never beheld
so delightful a prospect," wrote a wounded officer at
Albany a fortnight after.

Rogers with the rangers, and Gage with the light
infantry, led the way in whaleboats, followed by Bradstreet with his corps of boatmen, armed and drilled as
soldiers. Then came the main body. The central
column of regulars was commanded by Lord Howe, his
own regiment, the fifty-fifth, in the van, followed by the
Royal Americans, the twenty-seventh, forty-fourth, forty-
sixth, and eightieth infantry, and the Highlanders of the
forty-second, with their major, Duncan Campbell of

Inverawe, silent and gloomy amid the general cheer, for his soul was dark with foreshadowings of death. With this central column came what are described as two floating castles, which were no doubt batteries to cover the landing of the troops. On the right hand and the left were the provincials, uniformed in blue, regiment after regiment, from Massachusetts, Connecticut, New York, New Jersey, and Rhode Island. Behind them all came the bateaux, loaded with stores and baggage, and the heavy flat boats that carried the artillery, while a rear-guard of provincials and regulars closed the long procession.

At five in the afternoon they reached Sabbath-Day Point, twenty-five miles down the lake, where they stopped till late in the evening, waiting for the baggage and artillery, which had lagged behind; and here Lord Howe, lying on a bearskin by the side of the ranger, John Stark, questioned him as to the position of Ticonderoga and its best points of approach. At about eleven o'clock they set out again, and at daybreak entered what was then called the Second Narrows; that is to say, the contraction of the lake where it approaches its outlet. Close on their left, ruddy in the warm sunrise, rose the vast bare face of Rogers Rock, whence a French advanced party, under Langy and an officer named Trepezec, was watching their movements. Lord Howe, with Rogers and Bradstreet, went in whaleboats to reconnoitre the landing. At the place which the French called the Burned Camp, where Montcalm had embarked the summer before, they saw a detachment of the enemy too weak to oppose them. Their men landed and drove them off. At noon the whole army was on shore. Rogers, with a party of rangers, was ordered forward to reconnoitre, and the troops were formed for the march.

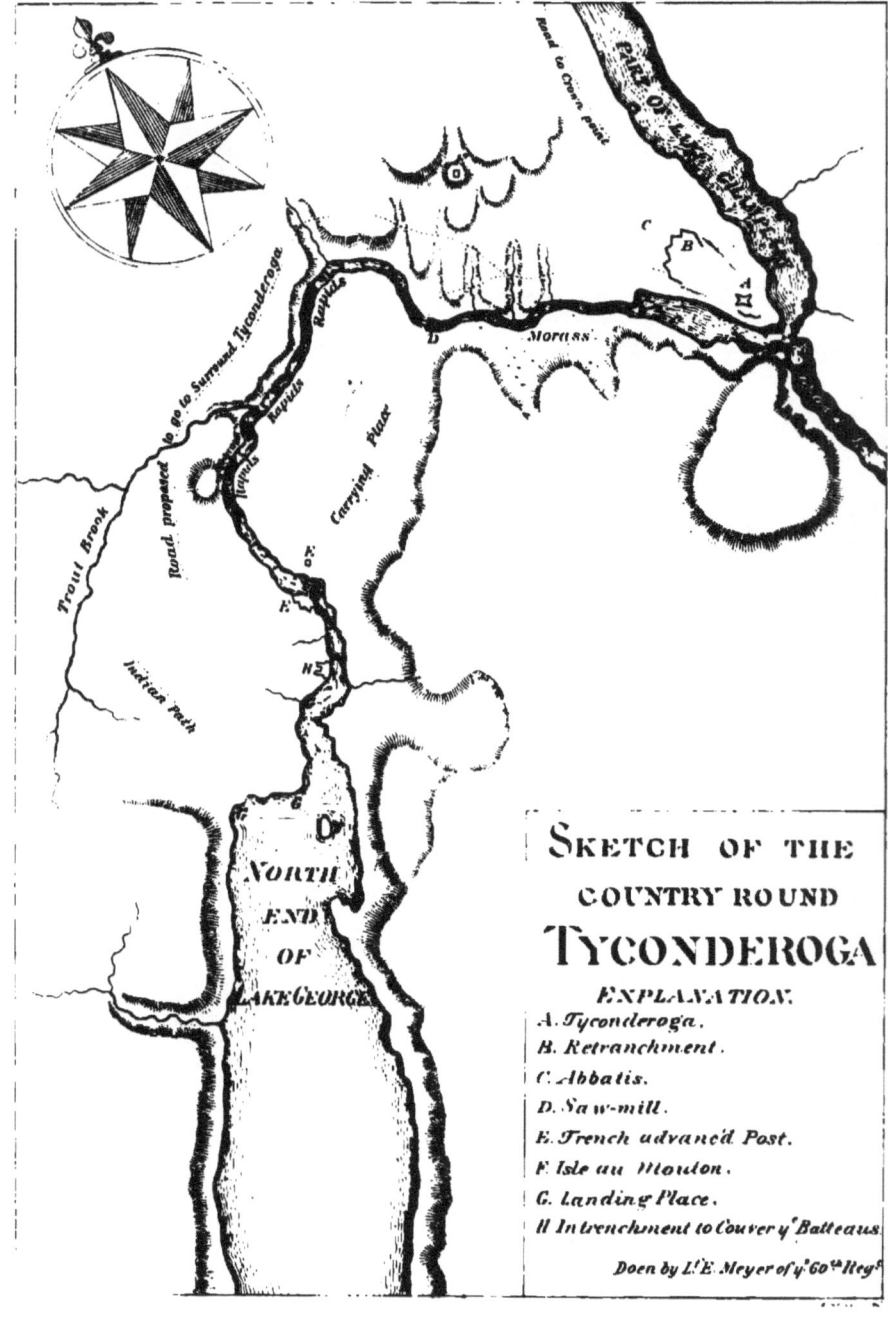

SKETCH OF THE
COUNTRY ROUND
TYCONDEROGA
EXPLANATION.

A. *Tyconderoga.*
B. *Retranchment.*
C. *Abbatis.*
D. *Saw-mill.*
E. *French advanc'd Post.*
F. *Isle au Mouton.*
G. *Landing Place.*
H. *Intrenchment to Couver y*. *Batteaus.*

Doen by L.t E. Meyer of y. 60.th Reg.t

From this part of the shore [1] a plain covered with
forest stretched northwestward half a mile or more to
the mountains behind which lay the valley of Trout
Brook.   On this plain the army began its march in four
columns, with the intention of passing round the western bank of the river of the outlet, since the bridge over
it had been destroyed.   Rogers, with the provincial
regiments of Fitch and Lyman, led the way, at some
distance before the rest.   The forest was extremely
dense and heavy, and so obstructed with undergrowth
that it was impossible to see more than a few yards in
any direction, while the ground was encumbered with
fallen trees in every stage of decay.   The ranks were
broken, and the men struggled on as they could in
dampness and shade, under a canopy of boughs that the
sun could scarcely pierce.   The difficulty increased
when, after advancing about a mile, they came upon
undulating and broken ground.   They were now not far
from the upper rapids of the outlet.   The guides became
bewildered in the maze of trunks and boughs; the
marching columns were confused, and fell in one upon
the other.   They were in the strange situation of an
army lost in the woods.

The advanced party of French under Langy and
Trepezee, about three hundred and fifty in all, regulars
and Canadians, had tried to retreat; but before they
could do so, the whole English army had passed them,
landed, and placed itself between them and their countrymen.   They had no resource but to take to the woods.
They seem to have climbed the steep gorge at the side
of Rogers Rock and followed the Indian path that led
to the valley of Trout Brook, thinking to descend it,
and, by circling along the outskirts of the valley of

[1] Between the old and new steamboat-landings, and parts adjacent.

Ticonderoga, reach Montcalm's camp at the saw-mill.
Langy was used to bushranging; but he too became perplexed in the blind intricacies of the forest. Towards the
close of the day he and his men had come out from the
valley of Trout Brook, and were near the junction of that
stream with the river of the outlet, in a state of some
anxiety, for they could see nothing but brown trunks and
green boughs. Could any of them have climbed one of
the great pines that here and there reared their shaggy
spires high above the surrounding forest, they would
have discovered where they were, but would have
gained not the faintest knowledge of the enemy. Out
of the woods on the right they would have seen a smoke
rising from the burning huts of the French camp at the
head of the portage, which Bourlamaque had set on fire
and abandoned. At a mile or more in front, the saw-
mill at the Falls might perhaps have been descried, and,
by glimpses between the trees, the tents of the neighboring camp where Montcalm still lay with his main force.
All the rest seemed lonely as the grave; mountain and
valley lay wrapped in primeval woods, and none could
have dreamed that, not far distant, an army was groping
its way, buried in foliage; no rumbling of wagons and
artillery trains, for none were there; all silent but the
cawing of some crow flapping his black wings over the
sea of tree-tops.

Lord Howe, with Major Israel Putnam and two hundred rangers, was at the head of the principal column,
which was a little in advance of the three others. Suddenly the challenge, *Qui vive!* rang sharply from the
thickets in front. *Français!* was the reply. Langy's
men were not deceived; they fired out of the bushes.
The shots were returned; a hot skirmish followed;
and Lord Howe dropped dead, shot through the breast.

All was confusion. The dull, vicious reports of musketry in thick woods, at first few and scattering, then in fierce and rapid volleys, reached the troops behind. They could hear, but see nothing. Already harassed and perplexed, they became perturbed. For all they knew, Montcalm's whole army was upon them. Nothing prevented a panic but the steadiness of the rangers, who maintained the fight alone till the rest came back to their senses. Rogers, with his reconnoitring party, and the regiments of Fitch and Lyman, were at no great distance in front. They all turned on hearing the musketry, and thus the French were caught between two fires. They fought with desperation. About fifty of them at length escaped; a hundred and forty-eight were captured, and the rest killed or drowned in trying to cross the rapids. The loss of the English was small in numbers, but immeasurable in the death of Howe. "The fall of this noble and brave officer," says Rogers, "seemed to produce an almost general languor and consternation through the whole army." "In Lord Howe," writes another contemporary, Major Thomas Mante, "the soul of General Abercromby's army seemed to expire. From the unhappy moment the General was deprived of his advice, neither order nor discipline was observed, and a strange kind of infatuation usurped the place of resolution." The death of one man was the ruin of fifteen thousand.

The evil news was despatched to Albany, and in two or three days the messenger who bore it passed the house of Mrs. Schuyler on the meadows above the town. "In the afternoon," says her biographer, "a man was seen coming from the north galloping violently without his hat. Pedrom, as he was familiarly called, Colonel Schuyler's only surviving brother, was with her, and ran

instantly to inquire, well knowing that he rode express.
The man galloped on, crying out that Lord Howe was
killed. The mind of our good aunt had been so engrossed by her anxiety and fears for the event impend-
ing, and so impressed with the merit and magnanimity
of her favorite hero, that her wonted firmness sank
under the stroke, and she broke out into bitter lamenta-
tions. This had such an effect on her friends and do-
mestics that shrieks and sobs of anguish echoed through
every part of the house."

The effect of the loss was seen at once. The army
was needlessly kept under arms all night in the forest,
and in the morning was ordered back to the landing
whence it came. Towards noon, however, Bradstreet
was sent with a detachment of regulars and provincials
to take possession of the saw-mill at the Falls, which
Montcalm had abandoned the evening before. Bradstreet rebuilt the bridges destroyed by the retiring
enemy, and sent word to his commander that the way
was open; on which Abercromby again put his army
in motion, reached the Falls late in the afternoon, and
occupied the deserted encampment of the French.

Montcalm with his main force had held this position
at the Falls through most of the preceding day, doubtful,
it seems, to the last whether he should not make his
final stand there. Bourlamaque was for doing so; but
two old officers, Bernès and Montguy, pointed out the
danger that the English would occupy the neighboring
heights; whereupon Montcalm at length resolved to fall
back. The camp was broken up at five o'clock. Some
of the troops embarked in bateaux, while others marched
a mile and a half along the forest road, passed the
place where the battalion of Berry was still at work on
the breastwork begun in the morning, and made their

bivouac a little farther on, upon the cleared ground that surrounded the fort.

The peninsula of Ticonderoga consists of a rocky plateau, with low grounds on each side, bordering Lake Champlain on the one hand, and the outlet of Lake George on the other. The fort stood near the end of the peninsula, which points towards the southeast. Thence, as one goes westward, the ground declines a little, and then slowly rises, till, about half a mile from the fort, it reaches its greatest elevation, and begins still more gradually to decline again. Thus a ridge is formed across the plateau between the steep declivities that sink to the low grounds on right and left. Some weeks before, a French officer named Hugues had suggested the defence of this ridge by means of an abatis. Montcalm approved his plan; and now, at the eleventh hour, he resolved to make his stand here. The two engineers, Pontleroy and Desandrouin, had already traced the outline of the works, and the soldiers of the battalion of Berry had made some progress in constructing them. At dawn of the seventh, while Abercromby, fortunately for his enemy, was drawing his troops back to the landing-place, the whole French army fell to their task. The regimental colors were planted along the line, and the officers, stripped to the shirt, took axe in hand and labored with their men. The trees that covered the ground were hewn down by thousands, the tops lopped off, and the trunks piled one upon another to form a massive breastwork. The line followed the top of the ridge, along which it zigzagged in such a manner that the whole front could be swept by flank fires of musketry and grape. Abercromby describes the wall of logs as between eight and nine feet high; in which case there must have been a rude *banquette*, or platform to fire from, on the inner side. It was certainly so high that nothing could be seen over it but the crowns of the soldiers' hats. The upper tier was formed of single logs, in which notches were cut to serve as loopholes; and in some places sods and bags of sand were piled along the top, with narrow spaces to fire through. From the central part of the line the ground sloped away like a natural glacis; while at the sides, and especially on the left, it was undulating and broken. Over this whole space, to the distance of a musket-shot from the works, the forest was cut down, and the trees left lying where they fell among the stumps, with tops turned outwards, forming one vast abatis, which, as a Massachusetts officer says, looked like a forest laid flat by a hurricane. But the most formidable obstruction was immediately along the front of the breastwork, where the ground was covered with heavy boughs, overlapping and interlaced, with sharpened points bristling into the face of the assailant like the quills of a porcupine. As these works were all of wood, no vestige of them remains. The earthworks now shown to tourists as the lines of Montcalm are of later construction; and though on the same ground, are not on the same plan.

Here, then, was a position which, if attacked in front with musketry alone, might be called impregnable. But would Abercromby so attack it? He had several alternatives. He might attempt the flank and rear of his enemy by way of the low grounds on the right and left of the plateau, a movement which the precautions of Montcalm had made difficult, but not impossible. Or, instead of leaving his artillery idle on the strand of Lake George, he might bring it to the front and batter the breastwork, which, though impervious to musketry, was worthless against heavy cannon. Or he might do what Burgoyne did with success a score of years later, and plant a battery on the heights of Rattlesnake Hill, now called Mount Defiance, which commanded the position of the French, and whence the inside of their breastwork could be scoured with round-shot from end to end. Or, while threatening the French front with a part of his army, he could march the rest a short distance through the woods on his left to the road which led from Ticonderoga to Crown Point, and which would soon have brought him to the place called Five-Mile Point, where Lake Champlain narrows to the width of an easy rifle-shot, and where a battery of field-pieces would have cut off all Montcalm's supplies and closed his only way of retreat. As the French were provisioned for but eight days, their position would thus have been desperate. They plainly saw the danger; and Doreil declares that had the movement been made, their whole army must have surrendered. Montcalm had done what he could; but the danger of his position was inevitable and extreme. His hope lay in Abercromby; and it was a hope well founded. The action of the English general answered the utmost wishes of his enemy.

Abercromby had been told by his prisoners that Montcalm had six thousand men, and that three thousand more were expected every hour. Therefore he was in haste to attack before these succors could arrive. As was the general, so was the army. "I believe," writes an officer, "we were one and all infatuated by a notion of carrying every obstacle by a mere *coup de mousqueterie*." Leadership perished with Lord Howe, and nothing. was left but blind, headlong valor.

Clerk, chief engineer, was sent to reconnoitre the French works from Mount Defiance; and came back with the report that, to judge from what he could see, they might be carried by assault. Then, without waiting to bring up his cannon, Abercromby prepared to storm the lines.

The French finished their breastwork and abatis on the evening of the seventh, encamped behind them, slung their kettles, and rested after their heavy toil. Lévis had not yet appeared; but at twilight one of his officers, Captain Pouchot, arrived with three hundred regulars, and announced that his commander would come before morning with a hundred more. The reinforcement, though small, was welcome, and Lévis was a host in himself. Pouchot was told that the army was half a mile off. Thither he repaired, made his report to Montcalm, and looked with amazement at the prodigious amount of work accomplished in one day. Lévis himself arrived in the course of the night, and approved the arrangement of the troops. They lay behind their lines till daybreak; then the drums beat, and they formed in order of battle. The battalions of La Sarre and Languedoc were posted on the left, under Bourlamaque, the first battalion of Berry with that of Royal Roussillon in the centre, under Montcalm, and those of La Reine, Béarn, and Guienne on the right, under Lévis. A detachment of volunteers occupied the low grounds between the breastwork and the outlet of Lake George; while, at the foot of the declivity on the side towards Lake Champlain, were stationed four hundred and fifty colony regulars and Canadians, behind an abatis which they had made for themselves; and as they were covered by the cannon of the fort, there was some hope that they would check any flank movement which the English might attempt on that side. Their posts being thus assigned, the men fell to work again to strengthen their defences. Including those who came with Lévis, the total force of effective soldiers was now thirty-six hundred.

Soon after nine o'clock a distant and harmless fire of small-arms began on the slopes of Mount Defiance. It came from a party of Indians who had just arrived with Sir William Johnson, and who, after amusing themselves in this manner for a time, remained for the rest of the day safe spectators of the fight. The soldiers worked undisturbed till noon, when volleys of musketry were heard from the forest in front. It was the English light troops driving in the French pickets. A cannon was fired as a signal to drop tools and form for battle. The white uniforms lined the breastwork in a triple row, with the grenadiers behind them as a reserve, and the second battalion of Berry watching the flanks and rear.

Meanwhile the English army had moved forward from its camp by the saw-mill. First came the rangers, the light infantry, and Bradstreet's armed boatmen, who, emerging into the open space, began a spattering fire. Some of the provincial troops followed, extending from left to right, and opening fire in turn; then the regulars, who had formed in columns of attack under cover of the forest, advanced their solid red masses into the sunlight, and passing through the intervals between the provincial regiments, pushed forward to the assault. Across the rough ground, with its maze of fallen trees whose leaves hung withering in the July sun, they could see the top of the breastwork, but not the men behind it; when, in an instant, all the line was obscured by a gush of smoke, a crash of exploding firearms tore the air, and grapeshot and musket-balls swept the whole space like a tempest; "a damnable fire," says an officer who heard them screaming about his ears. The English had been ordered to carry the works with the bayonet; but their ranks were broken by the obstructions through which they struggled in vain to force their way, and they soon began to fire in turn. The storm raged in full fury for an hour. The assailants pushed close to the breastwork; but there they were stopped by the bristling mass of sharpened branches, which they could not pass under the murderous cross-fires that swept them from front and flank. At length they fell back, exclaiming that the works were impregnable. Abercromby, who was at the saw-mill, a mile and a half in the rear, sent orders to attack again, and again they came on as before.

The scene was frightful: masses of infuriated men who could not go forward and would not go back; straining for an enemy they could not reach, and firing on an enemy they could not see; caught in the entanglement of fallen trees; tripped by briers, stumbling over logs, tearing through boughs; shouting, yelling, cursing, and pelted all the while with bullets that killed them by scores, stretched them on the ground, or hung them on jagged branches in strange attitudes of death. The provincials supported the regulars with spirit, and some of them forced their way to the foot of the wooden wall.

The French fought with the intrepid gayety of their nation, and shouts of *Vive le Roi!* and *Vive notre Général!* mingled with the din of musketry. Montcalm, with his coat off, for the day was hot, directed the defence of the centre, and repaired to any part of the line where the danger for the time seemed greatest. He is warm in praise of his enemy, and declares that between one and seven o'clock they attacked him six successive times. Early in the action Abercromby tried to turn the French left by sending twenty bateaux, filled with troops, down the outlet of Lake George. They were met by the fire of the volunteers stationed to defend the low grounds on that side, and, still advancing, came within range of the cannon of the fort, which sank two of them and drove back the rest.

A curious incident happened during one of the attacks. De Bassignac, a captain in the battalion of Royal Roussillon, tied his handkerchief to the end of a musket and waved it over the breastwork in defiance. The English mistook it for a sign of surrender, and came forward with all possible speed, holding their muskets crossed over their heads in both hands, and crying *Quarter*. The French made the same mistake; and thinking that their enemies were giving themselves up as prisoners, ceased firing, and mounted on the top of the breastwork to receive them. Captain Pouchot, astonished, as he says, to see them perched there, looked out to learn the cause, and saw that the enemy meant anything but surrender. Whereupon he shouted with all his might: " *Tirez! Tirez! Ne voyez-vous pas que ces gens-là vont vous enlever?*" The soldiers, still standing on the breastwork, instantly gave the English a volley, which killed some of them, and sent back the rest discomfited.

This was set to the account of Gallic treachery. "Another deceit the enemy put upon us," says a military letter-writer: "they raised their hats above the breastwork, which our people fired at; they having loopholes to fire through, and being covered by the sods, we did them little damage, except shooting their hats to pieces." In one of the last assaults a soldier of the Rhode Island regiment, William Smith, managed to get through all obstructions and ensconce himself close under the breastwork, where in the confusion he remained for a time unnoticed, improving his advantages meanwhile by shooting several Frenchmen. Being at length observed, a

6

soldier fired vertically down upon him and wounded him
severely, but not enough to prevent his springing up,
striking at one of his enemies over the top of the wall,
and braining him with his hatchet. A British officer
who saw the feat, and was struck by the reckless daring
of the man, ordered two regulars to bring him off;
which, covered by a brisk fire of musketry, they succeeded in doing. A letter from the camp two or three
weeks later reports him as in a fair way to recover,
being, says the writer, much braced and invigorated by
his anger against the French, on whom he was swearing
to have his revenge.

Toward five o'clock two English columns joined in a
most determined assault on the extreme right of the
French, defended by the battalions of Guienne and
Béarn. The danger for a time was imminent. Montcalm hastened to the spot with the reserves. The
assailants hewed their way to the foot of the breastwork:
and though again and again repulsed, they again and
again renewed the attack. The Highlanders fought with
stubborn and unconquerable fury. " Even those who
were mortally wounded," writes one of their lieutenants,
" cried to their companions not to lose a thought upon
them, but to follow their officers and mind the honor of
their country. Their ardor was such that it was difficult to bring them off." Their major, Campbell of
Inverawe, found his foreboding true. He received a
mortal shot, and his clansmen bore him from the field.
Twenty-five of their officers were killed or wounded, and
half the men fell under the deadly fire that poured from
the loopholes. Captain John Campbell and a few followers tore their way through the abatis, climbed the
breastwork, leaped down among the French, and were
bayoneted there.

As the colony troops and Canadians on the low ground were left undisturbed, Lévis sent them an order to make a sortie and attack the left flank of the charging columns. They accordingly posted themselves among the trees along the declivity, and fired upwards at the enemy, who presently shifted their position to the right, out of the line of shot. The assault still continued, but in vain; and at six there was another effort, equally fruitless. From this time till half-past seven a lingering fight was kept up by the rangers and other provincials, firing from the edge of the woods and from behind the stumps, bushes, and fallen trees in front of the lines. Its only objects were to cover their comrades, who were collecting and bringing off the wounded, and to protect the retreat of the regulars, who fell back in disorder to the Falls. As twilight came on, the last combatant withdrew, and none were left but the dead. Abercromby had lost in killed, wounded, and missing, nineteen hundred and forty-four officers and men. The loss of the French, not counting that of Langy's detachment, was three hundred and seventy-seven. Bourlamaque was dangerously wounded; Bougainville slightly; and the hat of Lévis was twice shot through.

Montcalm, with a mighty load lifted from his soul, passed along the lines, and gave the tired soldiers the thanks they nobly deserved. Beer, wine, and food were served out to them, and they bivouacked for the night on the level ground between the breastwork and the fort. The enemy had met a terrible rebuff; yet the danger was not over. Abercromby still had more than thirteen thousand men, and he might renew the attack with cannon. But, on the morning of the ninth, a band of volunteers who had gone out to watch him brought

back the report that he was in full retreat. The saw-
mill at the Falls was on fire, and the last English soldier was gone. On the morning of the tenth, Lévis,
with a strong detachment, followed the road to the
landing-place, and found signs that a panic had over-
taken the defeated troops. They had left behind several
hundred barrels of provisions and a large quantity of
baggage ; while in a marshy place that they had crossed
was found a considerable number of their shoes, which
had stuck in the mud, and which they had not stopped
to recover. They had embarked on the morning after
the battle, and retreated to the head of the lake in a
disorder and dejection wofully contrasted with the pomp
of their advance. A gallant army was sacrificed by the
blunders of its chief.

Montcalm announced his victory to his wife in a strain
of exaggeration that marks the exaltation of his mind.
" Without Indians, almost without Canadians or colony
troops, — I had only four hundred, — alone with Lévis
and Bourlamaque and the troops of the line, thirty-one
hundred fighting men, I have beaten an army of twenty-
five thousand. They repassed the lake precipitately,
with a loss of at least five thousand. This glorious day
does infinite honor to the valor of our battalions. I have
no time to write more. I am well, my dearest, and I
embrace you." And he wrote to his friend Doreil :
" The army, the too-small army of the King, has beaten
the enemy. What a day for France ! If I had had two
hundred Indians to send out at the head of a thousand
picked men under the Chevalier de Lévis, not many
would have escaped. Ah, my dear Doreil, what soldiers
are ours ! I never saw the like. Why were they not
at Louisbourg ? "

On the morrow of his victory he caused a great cross
to be planted on the battle-field, inscribed with these
lines, composed by the soldier-scholar himself,—

"Quid dux? quid miles? quid strata ingentia ligna?
"En Signum! en victor! Deus hic, Deus ipse triumphat."

"Soldier and chief and rampart's strength are nought;
Behold the conquering Cross! 'T is God the triumph wrought."

MENTION has been made of the death of Major Duncan Campbell of Inverawe. The following family tradition relating to it was told me in 1878 by the late Dean Stanley, to whom I am also indebted for various papers on the subject, including a letter from James Campbell, Esq., the present laird of Inverawe, and great-nephew of the hero of the tale. The same story is told, in an amplified form and with some variations, in the *Legendary Tales of the Highlands* of Sir Thomas Dick Lauder. As related by Dean Stanley and approved by Mr. Campbell, it is this : —

The ancient castle of Inverawe stands by the banks of the Awe, in the midst of the wild and picturesque scenery of the western Highlands. Late one evening, before the middle of the last century, as the laird, Duncan Campbell, sat alone in the old hall, there was a loud knocking at the gate; and, opening it, he saw a stranger, with torn clothing and kilt besmeared with blood, who in a breathless voice begged for asylum. He went on to say that he had killed a man in a fray, and that the pursuers were at his heels. Campbell promised to shelter him. "Swear on your dirk!" said the stranger; and Campbell swore. He then led him to a secret recess in the depths of the castle. Scarcely was he hidden when again there was a loud knocking at the gate, and two armed men appeared. " Your cousin Donald has been murdered, and we are looking for the murderer!" Campbell, remembering his oath, professed to have no knowledge of the fugitive; and the men went on their way. The laird, in great agitation, lay down to rest in a large dark room, where at length he fell asleep. Waking suddenly in bewilderment and terror, he saw the ghost of the murdered Donald standing by his bedside, and heard a hollow voice pronounce the words: " *Inverawe! Inverawe! blood has been shed. Shield not the murderer!* " In the morning Campbell went to the hiding-place of the guilty man and told him that he could harbor him no longer. " You have sworn on your dirk!" he replied; and the laird of Inverawe, greatly perplexed and troubled, made a compromise between conflicting duties, promised not to betray his guest, led him to the neighboring mountain, and hid him in a cave.

In the next night, as he lay tossing in feverish slumbers, the same stern voice awoke him, the ghost of his cousin Donald stood again at his bedside, and again he heard the same appalling words: " *Inverawe! Inverawe! blood has been shed. Shield not the murderer!* " At break of day he hastened, in strange agitation, to the cave; but it was empty, the stranger was gone. At night, as he strove in vain to sleep, the vision appeared once more, ghastly pale, but less stern of aspect than before. " *Farewell, Inverawe!* " it said; " *Farewell, till we meet at TICONDEROGA!* "

The strange name dwelt in Campbell's memory. He had joined the Black Watch, or Forty-second Regiment, then employed in keeping order in the turbulent Highlands. In time he became its major; and, a year or two after the war broke out, he went with it to America. Here, to his horror, he learned that it was ordered to the attack of Ticonderoga. His story was well known among his brother officers. They combined among themselves to disarm his fears; and when they reached the fatal spot they told him on the eve of the battle, "This is not Ticonderoga; we are not there yet; this is Fort George." But in the morning he came to them with haggard looks. "I have seen him! You have deceived me! He came to my tent last night! This is Ticonderoga! I shall die to-day!" and his prediction was fulfilled.

Such is the tradition. The indisputable facts are that Major Duncan Campbell of Inverawe, his arm shattered by a bullet, was carried to Fort Edward, where, after amputation, he died and was buried. (*Abercromby to Pitt*, 19 *August*, 1758.) The stone that marks his grave may still be seen, with this inscription: "*Here lyes the Body of Duncan Campbell of Inverawe, Esqre., Major to the old Highland Regiment, aged 55 Years, who died the 17th July, 1758, of the Wounds he received in the Attack of the Retrenchment of Ticonderoga or Carrillon, on the 8th July, 1758.*"

His son, Lieutenant Alexander Campbell, was severely wounded at the same time, but reached Scotland alive, and died in Glasgow.

Mr. Campbell, the present Inverawe, in the letter mentioned above, says that forty-five years ago he knew an old man whose grandfather was foster-brother to the slain major of the forty-second, and who told him the following story while carrying a salmon for him to an inn near Inverawe. The old man's grandfather was sleeping with his son, then a lad, in the same room, but in another bed. This son, father of the narrator, "was awakened," to borrow the words of Mr. Campbell, "by some unaccustomed sound, and behold there was a bright light in the room, and he saw a figure, in full Highland regimentals, cross over the room and stoop down over his father's bed and give him a kiss. He was too frightened to speak, but put his head under his coverlet and went to sleep. Once more he was roused in like manner, and saw the same sight. In the morning he spoke to his father about it, who told him that it was Macdonnochie [*the Gaelic patronymic of the laird of Inverawe*] whom he had seen, and who came to tell him that he had been killed in a great battle in America. Sure enough, said my informant, it was on the very day that the battle of Ticonderoga was fought and the laird was killed."

It is also said that two ladies of the family of Inverawe saw a battle in the clouds, in which the shadowy forms of Highland warriors were plainly to be descried; and that when the fatal news came from America, it was found that the time of the vision answered exactly to that of the battle in which the head of the family fell.

NIAGARA.

SIEGE OF FORT NIAGARA.

THE River Niagara was known to the Jesuits as early as 1640. The Falls are indicated on Champlain's map of 1632, and in 1648 the Jesuit Ruguencau speaks of them as a "cataract of frightful height."

In 1678, the Falls were visited by the friar Louis Hennepin, who gives an exaggerated description of them, and illustrates it by a curious picture. The name Niagara is of Iroquois origin, and in the Mohawk dialect is pronounced Nyàgarah.

In the year of Hennepin's visit, the followers of Cavelier de la Salle began a fortified storehouse where Lewiston now stands, and on Cayuga Creek, a few miles above the Falls, La Salle built the "Griffin," the first vessel that ever sailed on the Upper Lakes. At the same time he began a fort at the mouth of the river. La Salle's fort fell to ruin, and another was built in its place a few years after. This, too, was abandoned to be again rebuilt, and the post remained in French hands more than half a century. It was of the greatest importance, since it commanded the chief route from Canada to the interior of the continent. At length, in 1759, the year of Wolfe's famous victory at Quebec, General Prideaux was sent to reduce it.

Prideaux safely reached Niagara, and laid siege to it. Fort Niagara was a strong work, lately rebuilt in regular form by an excellent officer, Captain Pouchot, of the battalion of Béarn, who commanded it. It stood where the present fort stands, in the angle formed by the junction of the River Niagara with Lake Ontario, and was held by about six hundred men, well supplied with provisions and munitions of war. Higher up the river, a mile and a half above the cataract, there was another fort, called Little Niagara, built of wood, and commanded by the half-breed officer, Joncaire-Chabert, who with his brother, Joncaire-Clauzonne, and a numerous clan of Indian relatives, had long thwarted the efforts of Sir William Johnson to engage the Five Nations in the English cause. But recent English successes had had their effect. Joncaire's influence was waning, and Johnson was now in Prideaux's camp with nine hundred Five Nation warriors pledged to fight the French. Joncaire, finding his fort untenable, burned it, and came with his garrison and his Indian friends to reinforce Niagara.

Pouchot had another resource, on which he confidently relied. In obedience to an order from Vaudreuil, the French population of the Illinois, Detroit, and other distant posts, joined with troops of Western Indians, had come down the Lakes to restore French ascendency on the Ohio. These mixed bands of white men and red, bushrangers and savages, were now gathered, partly at Le Bœuf and Venango, but chiefly at Presquisle, under command of Aubry, Ligneris, Marin, and other partisan chiefs, the best in Canada. No sooner did Pouchot learn that the English were coming to attack him than he sent a messenger to summon them all to his aid.

The siege was begun in form, though the English engineers were so incompetent that the trenches, as first laid out, were scoured by the fire of the place, and had to be made anew. At last the batteries opened fire. A shell from a cochorn burst prematurely, just as it left the mouth of the piece, and a fragment striking Prideaux on the head, killed him instantly. Johnson took command in his place, and made up in energy what he lacked in skill. In two or three weeks the fort was in extremity. The rampart was breached, more than a hundred of the garrison were killed or disabled, and the rest were exhausted with want of sleep. Pouchot watched anxiously for the promised succors; and on the morning of the twenty-fourth of July a distant firing told him that they were at hand.

Aubry and Ligneris, with their motley following, had left Presquisle a few days before, to the number, according to Vaudreuil, of eleven hundred French and two hundred Indians. Among them was a body of colony troops; but the Frenchmen of the party were chiefly traders and bushrangers from the West, connecting links between civilization and savagery; some of them indeed were mere white Indians, imbued with the ideas and morals of the wigwam, wearing hunting-shirts of smoked deer-skin embroidered with quills of the Canada porcupine, painting their faces black and red, tying eagle feathers in their long hair, or plastering it on their temples with a compound of vermilion and glue. They were excellent woodsmen, skilful hunters, and perhaps the best bushfighters in all Canada.

When Pouchot heard the firing, he went with a wounded artillery officer to the bastion next the river; and as the forest had been cut away for a great distance, they could see more than a mile and a half along the shore. There, by glimpses among trees and bushes, they descried bodies of men, now advancing, and now retreating; Indians in rapid movement, and the smoke

of guns, the sound of which reached their ears in heavy
volleys, or a sharp and angry rattle. Meanwhile the
English cannon had ceased their fire, and the silent
trenches seemed deserted, as if their occupants were
gone to meet the advancing foe. There was a call in
the fort for volunteers to sally and destroy the works;
but no sooner did they show themselves along the
covered way than the seemingly abandoned trenches
were thronged with men and bayonets, and the attempt
was given up. The distant firing lasted half an hour,
then ceased, and Pouchot remained in suspense; till, at
two in the afternoon, a friendly Onondaga, who had
passed unnoticed through the English lines, came to
him with the announcement that the French and their
allies had been routed and cut to pieces. Pouchot would
not believe him.

Nevertheless his tale was true. Johnson, besides his
Indians, had with him about twenty-three hundred men,
whom he was forced to divide into three separate bodies,
— one to guard the bateaux, one to guard the trenches,
and one to fight Aubry and his band. This last body
consisted of the provincial light infantry and the pickets,
two companies of grenadiers, and a hundred and fifty
men of the forty-sixth regiment, all under command of
Colonel Massey. They took post behind an abatis at a
place called La Belle Famille, and the Five Nation warriors placed themselves on their flanks. These savages
had shown signs of disaffection; and when the enemy
approached, they opened a parley with the French
Indians, which, however, soon ended, and both sides
raised the war-whoop. The fight was brisk for a while;
but at last Aubry's men broke away in a panic. The
French officers seem to have made desperate efforts to
retrieve the day, for nearly all of them were killed or

captured; while their followers, after heavy loss, fled to their canoes and boats above the cataract, hastened back to Lake Erie, burned Presquisle, Le Bœuf, and Venango, and, joined by the garrisons of those forts, retreated to Detroit, leaving the whole region of the upper Ohio in undisputed possession of the English.

At four o'clock on the day of the battle, after a furious cannonade on both sides, a trumpet sounded from the trenches, and an officer approached the fort with a summons to surrender. He brought also a paper containing the names of the captive French officers, though some of them were spelled in a way that defied recognition. Pouchot, feigning incredulity, sent an officer of his own to the English camp, who soon saw unanswerable proof of the disaster; for here, under a shelter of leaves and boughs near the tent of Johnson, sat Ligneris, severely wounded, with Aubry, Villiers, Montigny, Marin, and their companions in misfortune,—in all, sixteen officers, four cadets, and a surgeon.

Pouchot had now no choice but surrender. By the terms of the capitulation, the garrison were to be sent prisoners to New York, though honors of war were granted them in acknowledgment of their courageous conduct. There was a special stipulation that they should be protected from the Indians, of whom they stood in the greatest terror, lest the massacre of Fort William Henry should be avenged upon them. Johnson restrained his dangerous allies, and, though the fort was pillaged, no blood was shed.

The capture of Niagara was an important stroke. Thenceforth Detroit, Michillimackinac, the Illinois, and all the other French interior posts were severed from Canada and left in helpless isolation. The conquest of the whole interior became only a question of time.

7

MASSACRE OF THE DEVIL'S HOLE.

AFTER the conquest of Canada, there was a general uprising of the Indian tribes, led by the famous Pontiac, against the British forts and settlements. In the war that followed, a remarkable incident took place a little way below Niagara Falls.

The carrying-place of Niagara formed an essential link in the chain of communication between the province of New York and the interior country. Men and military stores were conveyed in boats up the river, as far as the present site of Lewiston. Thence a portage road, several miles in length, passed along the banks of the stream, and terminated at Fort Schlosser, above the cataract. This road traversed a region whose sublime features have gained for it a world-wide renown. The River Niagara, a short distance below the cataract, assumes an aspect scarcely less remarkable than that stupendous scene itself. Its channel is formed by a vast ravine, whose sides, now bare and weather-stained, now shaggy with forest-trees, rise in cliffs of appalling height and steepness. Along this chasm pour all the waters of the lakes, heaving their furious surges with the power of an ocean and the rage of a mountain torrent. About three miles below the cataract, the precipices which form the eastern wall of the ravine are broken by an abyss of awful depth and blackness, bearing at the present day the name of the Devil's Hole. In its shallowest part, the precipice sinks sheer down to the depth of eighty feet, where it meets a chaotic mass of rocks, descending with an abrupt declivity to unseen depths below. Within the cold and damp recesses of the gulf, a host of forest-trees have rooted themselves; and, standing on the perilous brink, one may look down upon the mingled foliage of ash, poplar, and maple, while, above them all, the spruce and fir shoot their sharp and rigid spires upward into sunlight. The roar of the convulsed river swells heavily on the ear, and, far below, its headlong waters may be discerned careering in foam past the openings of the matted foliage.

On the thirteenth of September, 1763, a numerous train of wagons and pack horses proceeded from the lower landing to Fort Schlosser, and on the following morning set out on their return, guarded by an escort of twenty-four soldiers. They pursued their slow progress until they reached a point where the road passed along the brink of the Devil's Hole. The gulf yawned on their left, while on their right the road was skirted by low and densely wooded hills. Suddenly they were greeted by the blaze and clatter of a hundred rifles. Then followed the startled cries of men, and the bounding of maddened horses. At the next instant, a host of Indians broke screeching from the woods, and rifle-but and tomahawk finished the bloody work. All was over in a moment. Horses leaped the precipice; men were driven shrieking into the abyss; teams and wagons went over, crashing to atoms among the rocks below. Tradition relates that the drummer boy of the detachment was caught, in his fall, among the branches of a tree, where he hung suspended by his drum-strap. Being but slightly injured, he disengaged himself, and, hiding in the recesses of the gulf, finally escaped. One of the teamsters also, who was wounded at the first fire, contrived to crawl into the woods, where he lay concealed till the Indians had left the place. Besides these two, the only survivor was Stedman, the conductor of the convoy, who, being well mounted, and seeing the whole party forced helplessly towards the precipice, wheeled his horse, and resolutely spurred through the crowd of Indians. One of them, it is said, seized his bridle; but he freed himself by a dexterous use of his knife, and plunged into the woods, untouched by the bullets which whistled about his head. Flying at full speed through the forest, he reached Fort Schlosser in safety.

The distant sound of the Indian rifles had been heard by a party of soldiers, who occupied a small fortified camp near the lower landing. Forming in haste, they advanced eagerly to the rescue. In anticipation of this movement, the Indians, who were nearly five hundred in number, had separated into two parties, one of which had stationed itself at the Devil's Hole, to waylay the convoy, while the other formed an ambuscade upon the road a mile nearer the landing-place. The soldiers, marching precipitately, and huddled in a close body, were suddenly assailed by a volley of rifles, which stretched half their number dead upon the road. Then, rushing from the forest, the Indians cut down the survivors with merciless ferocity. A small remnant only escaped the massacre, and fled to Fort Niagara with the tidings. Major Wilkins, who commanded at this post, lost no time in marching to the spot, with nearly the whole strength of his garrison. Not an Indian was to be found. At the two places of ambuscade, about seventy dead bodies were counted, naked, scalpless, and so horribly mangled that many of them could not be recognized. All the wagons had been broken to pieces, and such of the horses as were not driven over the precipice had been carried off, laden, doubtless, with the plunder. The ambuscade of the Devil's Hole has gained a traditionary immortality, adding fearful interest to a scene whose native horrors need no aid from the imagination.

MONTREAL.

THE BIRTH OF MONTREAL.

WE come now to an enterprise as singular in its character as it proved important in its results.

At La Flèche, in Anjou, dwelt one Jérôme le Royer de la Dauversière, receiver of taxes. His portrait shows us a round, *bourgeois* face, somewhat heavy perhaps, decorated with a slight mustache, and redeemed by bright and earnest eyes. On his head he wears a black skull-cap; and over his ample shoulders spreads a stiff white collar, of wide expanse and studious plainness. Though he belonged to the *noblesse*, his look is that of a grave burgher, of good renown and sage deportment. Dauversière was, however, an enthusiastic devotee, of mystical tendencies, who whipped himself with a scourge of small chains till his shoulders were one wound, wore a belt with more than twelve hundred sharp points, and invented for himself other torments, which filled his confessor with admiration. One day, while at his devotions, he heard an inward voice commanding him to become the founder of a new Order of hospital nuns; and he was further ordered to establish, on the island called Montreal, in Canada, a hospital, or Hôtel-Dieu, to be conducted by these nuns. But Montreal was a wilderness, and the hospital would have no patients. Therefore, in order to supply them, the island must first be colonized. Dauversière was greatly perplexed. On the one hand, the voice of Heaven must be obeyed;

on the other, he had a wife, six children, and a very moderate fortune.

Again : there was at Paris a young priest, about twenty-eight years of age, — Jean Jacques Olier, afterwards widely known as founder of the Seminary of St. Sulpice. Judged by his engraved portrait, his countenance, though marked both with energy and intellect, was anything but prepossessing. Every lineament proclaims the priest. Yet the Abbé Olier has high titles to esteem. He signalized his piety, it is true, by the most disgusting exploits of self-mortification ; but, at the same time, he was strenuous in his efforts to reform the people and the clergy. So zealous was he for good morals, that he drew upon himself the imputation of a leaning to the heresy of the Jansenists, — a suspicion strengthened by his opposition to certain priests, who, to secure the faithful in their allegiance, justified them in lives of licentiousness. Yet Olier's catholicity was past attaintment, and in his horror of Jansenists he yielded to the Jesuits alone.

He was praying in the ancient church of St. Germain des Prés, when, like Dauversière, he thought he heard a voice from Heaven, saying that he was destined to be a light to the Gentiles. It is recorded as a mystic coincidence attending this miracle, that the choir was at that very time chanting the words, *Lumen ad revelationem Gentium ;* and it seems to have occurred neither to Olier nor to his biographer, that, falling on the ear of the rapt worshipper, they might have unconsciously suggested the supposed revelation. But there was a further miracle. An inward voice told Olier that he was to form a society of priests, and establish them on the island called Montreal, in Canada, for the propagation of the True Faith ; and writers old and recent

assert, that, while both he and Dauversière were totally
ignorant of Canadian geography, they suddenly found
themselves in possession, they knew not how, of the
most exact details concerning Montreal, its size, shape,
situation, soil, climate, and productions.

The annual volumes of the Jesuit *Relations*, issuing
from the renowned press of Cramoisy, were at this time
spread broadcast throughout France ; and, in the circles
of *haute devotion*, Canada and its missions were everywhere the themes of enthusiastic discussion ; while
Champlain, in his published works, had long before
pointed out Montreal as the proper site for a settlement.
But we are entering a region of miracle, and it is super-
fluous to look far for explanations. The illusion, in
these cases, is a part of the history.

Dauversière pondered the revelation he had received ;
and the more he pondered, the more was he convinced
that it came from God. He therefore set out for Paris,
to find some means of accomplishing the task assigned
him. Here, as he prayed before an image of the Virgin
in the church of Notre-Dame, he fell into an ecstasy,
and beheld a vision. "I should be false to the integrity
of history," writes his biographer, "if I did not relate
it here." And he adds, that the reality of this celestial
favor is past doubting, inasmuch as Dauversière himself
told it to his daughters. Christ, the Virgin, and St.
Joseph appeared before him. He saw them distinctly.
Then he heard Christ ask three times of his Virgin
Mother, *Where can I find a faithful servant ?* On which,
the Virgin, taking him (Dauversière) by the hand,
replied, *See, Lord, here is that faithful servant !* — and
Christ, with a benignant smile, received him into his service, promising to bestow on him wisdom and strength to
do his work. From Paris he went to the neighboring

château of Meudon, which overlooks the valley of the Seine, not far from St. Cloud. Entering the gallery of the old castle, he saw a priest approaching him. It was Olier. Now we are told that neither of these men had ever seen or heard of the other; and yet, says the pious historian, "impelled by a kind of inspiration, they know each other at once, even to the depths of their hearts; saluted each other by name, as we read of St. Paul, the Hermit, and St. Anthony, and of St. Dominic and St. Francis; and ran to embrace each other, like two friends who had met after a long separation."

"Monsieur," exclaimed Olier, "I know your design, and I go to commend it to God at the holy altar."

And he went at once to say mass in the chapel. Dauversière received the communion at his hands; and then they walked for three hours in the park, discussing their plans. They were of one mind, in respect both to objects and means; and when they parted, Olier gave Dauversière a hundred louis, saying, "This is to begin the work of God."

They proposed to found at Montreal three religious communities, — *three* being the mystic number, — one of secular priests to direct the colonists and convert the Indians, one of nuns to nurse the sick, and one of nuns to teach the Faith to the children, white and red. To borrow their own phrases, they would plant the banner of Christ in an abode of desolation and a haunt of demons; and to this end a band of priests and women were to invade the wilderness, and take post between the fangs of the Iroquois. But first they must make a colony, and to do so must raise money. Olier had pious and wealthy penitents; Dauversière had a friend, the Baron de Fancamp, devout as himself and far richer. Anxious for his soul, and satisfied that the enterprise was an inspiration of God, he was eager to bear part in it. Olier soon found three others; and the six together formed the germ of the Society of Notre-Dame de Montreal. Among them they raised the sum of seventy-five thousand livres, equivalent to about as many dollars at the present day.

Now to look for a moment at their plan. Their eulogists say, and with perfect truth, that, from a worldly point of view, it was mere folly. The partners mutually bound themselves to seek no return for the money expended. Their profit was to be reaped in the skies: and, indeed, there was none to be reaped on earth. The feeble settlement at Quebec was at this time in danger of utter ruin; for the Iroquois, enraged at the attacks made on them by Champlain, had begun a fearful course of retaliation, and the very existence of the colony trembled in the balance. But if Quebec was exposed to their ferocious inroads, Montreal was incomparably more so. A settlement here would be a perilous outpost, — a hand thrust into the jaws of the tiger. It would provoke attack, and lie almost in the path of the war-parties. The Associates could gain nothing by the fur-trade; for they would not be allowed to share in it. On the other hand, danger apart, the place was an excellent one for a mission; for here met two great rivers: the St. Lawrence, with its countless tributaries, flowed in from the west, while the Ottawa descended from the north; and Montreal, embraced by their uniting waters, was the key to a vast inland navigation. Thither the Indians would naturally resort; and thence the missionaries could make their way into the heart of a boundless heathendom. None of the ordinary motives of colonization had part in this design. It owed its conception and its birth to religious zeal alone.

The island of Montreal belonged to Lauson, former president of the great company of the Hundred Associates; and his son had a monopoly of fishing in the St. Lawrence. Dauversière and Fancamp, after much diplomacy, succeeded in persuading the elder Lauson to transfer his title to them; and, as there was a defect in it, they also obtained a grant of the island from the Hundred Associates, its original owners, who, however, reserved to themselves its western extremity as a site for a fort and storehouses. At the same time, the younger Lauson granted them a right of fishery within two leagues of the shores of the island, for which they were to make a yearly acknowledgment of ten pounds of fish. A confirmation of these grants was obtained from the King. Dauversière and his companions were now *seigneurs* of Montreal. They were empowered to appoint a governor, and to establish courts, from which there was to be an appeal to the Supreme Court of Quebec, supposing such to exist. They were excluded from the fur-trade, and forbidden to build castles or forts other than such as were necessary for defence against the Indians.

Their title assured, they matured their plan. First they would send out forty men to take possession of Montreal, intrench themselves, and raise crops. Then they would build a house for the priests, and two convents for the nuns. Meanwhile, Olier was toiling at Vaugirard, on the outskirts of Paris, to inaugurate the seminary of priests, and Dauversière at La Flèche, to form the community of hospital nuns. How the school nuns were provided for we shall see hereafter. The colony, it will be observed, was for the convents, not the convents for the colony.

The Associates needed a soldier-governor to take

charge of their forty men; and, directed as they supposed by Providence, they found one wholly to their mind. This was Paul de Chomedey, Sieur de Maisonneuve, a devout and valiant gentleman, who in long service among the heretics of Holland had kept his faith intact, and had held himself resolutely aloof from the license that surrounded him. He loved his profession of arms, and wished to consecrate his sword to the Church. Past all comparison, he is the manliest figure that appears in this group of zealots. The piety of the design, the miracles that inspired it, the adventure and the peril, all combined to charm him; and he eagerly embraced the enterprise. His father opposed his purpose; but he met him with a text of St. Mark, "There is no man that hath left house or brethren or sisters or father for my sake, but he shall receive an hundred-fold." On this the elder Maisonneuve, deceived by his own worldliness, imagined that the plan covered some hidden speculation, from which enormous profits were expected, and therefore withdrew his opposition.

Their scheme was ripening fast, when both Olier and Dauversière were assailed by one of those revulsions of spirit, to which saints of the ecstatic school are naturally liable. Dauversière, in particular, was a prey to the extremity of dejection, uncertainty, and misgiving. What had he, a family man, to do with ventures beyond sea? Was it not his first duty to support his wife and children? Could he not fulfil all his obligations as a Christian by reclaiming the wicked and relieving the poor at La Flèche? Plainly, he had doubts that his vocation was genuine. If we could raise the curtain of his domestic life, perhaps we should find him beset by wife and daughters, tearful and wrathful, inveighing against his folly, and imploring him to provide a support for them before squandering his money to plant a convent of nuns in a wilderness. How long his fit of dejection lasted does not appear; but at length he set himself again to his appointed work. Olier, too, emerging from the clouds and darkness, found faith once more, and again placed himself at the head of the great enterprise.

There was imperative need of more money; and Dauversière, under judicious guidance, was active in obtaining it. This miserable victim of illusions had a squat, uncourtly figure, and was no proficient in the graces either of manners or of speech: hence his success in commending his objects to persons of rank and wealth is set down as one of the many miracles which attended the birth of Montreal. But zeal and earnestness are in themselves a power; and the ground had been well marked out and ploughed for him in advance. That attractive, though intricate, subject of study, the female mind, has always engaged the attention of priests, more especially in countries where as in France, women exert a strong social and political influence. The art of kindling the flames of zeal, and the more difficult art of directing and controlling them, have been themes of reflection the most diligent and profound. Accordingly we find that a large proportion of the money raised for this enterprise was contributed by devout ladies. Many of them became members of the Association of Montreal, which was eventually increased to about forty-five persons, chosen for their devotion and their wealth.

Olier and his associates had resolved, though not from any collapse of zeal, to postpone the establishment of the seminary and the college until after a settlement should be formed. The hospital, however, might, they thought, be begun at once; for blood and blows would

be the assured portion of the first settlers. At least, a
discreet woman ought to embark with the first colonists
as their nurse and housekeeper. Scarcely was the need
recognized when it was supplied.

Mademoiselle Jeanne Mance was born of an honorable
family of Nogent-le-Roi, and in 1640 was thirty-four
years of age. These Canadian heroines began their religious experiences early. Of Marie de l'Incarnation we
read, that at the age of seven Christ appeared to her
in a vision; and the biographer of Mademoiselle Mance
assures us, with admiring gravity, that, at the same tender age, she bound herself to God by a vow of perpetual
chastity. This singular infant in due time became a
woman, of a delicate constitution, and manners graceful,
yet dignified. Though an earnest devotee, she felt no
vocation for the cloister; yet, while still " in the world,"
she led the life of a nun. The Jesuit *Relations*, and the
example of Madame de la Peltrie, of whom she had
heard, inoculated her with the Canadian enthusiasm,
then so prevalent; and, under the pretence of visiting
relatives, she made a journey to Paris, to take counsel
of certain priests. Of one thing she was assured: the
Divine will called her to Canada, but to what end she
neither knew nor asked to know; for she abandoned
herself as an atom to be borne to unknown destinies on
the breath of God. At Paris, Father St. Jure, a Jesuit,
assured her that her vocation to Canada was, past
doubt, a call from Heaven; while Father Rapin, a Ré-
collet, spread abroad the fame of her virtues, and introduced her to many ladies of rank, wealth, and zeal.
Then, well supplied with money for any pious work to
which she might be summoned, she journeyed to Rochelle, whence ships were to sail for New France. Thus
far she had been kept in ignorance of the plan with

regard to Montreal; but now Father La Place, a Jesuit, revealed it to her. On the day after her arrival at Rochelle, as she entered the Church of the Jesuits, she met Dauversière coming out. "Then," says her biographer, "these two persons, who had never seen nor heard of each other, were enlightened supernaturally, whereby their most hidden thoughts were mutually made known, as had happened already with M. Olier and this same M. de la Dauversière." A long conversation ensued between them; and the delights of this interview were never effaced from the mind of Mademoiselle Mance. "She used to speak of it like a seraph," writes one of her nuns, "and far better than many a learned doctor could have done."

She had found her destiny. The ocean, the wilderness, the solitude, the Iroquois,—nothing daunted her. She would go to Montreal with Maisonneuve and his forty men. Yet, when the vessel was about to sail, a new and sharp misgiving seized her. How could she, a woman, not yet bereft of youth or charms, live alone in the forest, among a troop of soldiers? Her scruples were relieved by two of the men, who, at the last moment, refused to embark without their wives,— and by a young woman, who, impelled by enthusiasm, escaped from her friends, and took passage, in spite of them, in one of the vessels.

All was ready; the ships set sail; but Olier, Dauversière, and Fancamp remained at home, as did also the other Associates, with the exception of Maisonneuve and Mademoiselle Mance. In the following February, an impressive scene took place in the Church of Notre-Dame, at Paris. The Associates, at this time numbering about forty-five, with Olier at their head, assembled before the altar of the Virgin, and, by a solemn ceremonial, consecrated Montreal to the Holy Family. Henceforth it was to be called *Villemarie de Montreal*, — a sacred town, reared to the honor and under the patronage of Christ, St. Joseph, and the Virgin, to be typified by three persons on earth, founders respectively of the three destined communities, — Olier, Dauversière, and a maiden of Troyes, Marguerite Bourgeoys: the seminary to be consecrated to Christ, the Hôtel-Dieu to St. Joseph, and the college to the Virgin.

But we are anticipating a little ; for it was several years as yet before Marguerite Bourgeoys took an active part in the work of Montreal. She was the daughter of a respectable tradesman, and was now twenty-two years of age. Her portrait has come down to us ; and her face is a mirror of loyalty and womanly tenderness. Her qualities were those of good sense, conscientiousness, and a warm heart. She had known no miracles, ecstasies, or trances ; and though afterwards, when her religious susceptibilities had reached a fuller development, a few such are recorded of her, yet even the Abbé Faillon, with the best intentions, can credit her with but a meagre allowance of these celestial favors. Though in the midst of visionaries, she distrusted the supernatural, and avowed her belief, that, in His government of the world, God does not often set aside its ordinary laws. Her religion was of the affections, and was manifested in an absorbing devotion to duty. She had felt no vocation to the cloister, but had taken the vow of chastity, and was attached, as an *externe*, to the Sisters of the Congregation of Troyes, who were fevered with eagerness to go to Canada. Marguerite, however, was content to wait until there was a prospect that she could do good by going ; and it was not till the year 1653, that, renouncing an inheritance, and giving all she had to the

poor, she embarked for the savage scene of her labors.
To this day, in crowded school-rooms of Montreal and
Quebec, fit monuments of her unobtrusive virtue, her
successors instruct the children of the poor, and embalm
the pleasant memory of Marguerite Bourgeoys. In the
martial figure of Maisonneuve, and the fair form of this
gentle nun, we find the true heroes of Montreal.

Maisonneuve, with his forty men and four women,
reached Quebec too late to ascend to Montreal that
season. They encountered distrust, jealousy, and opposition. The agents of the Company of the Hundred
Associates looked on them askance; and the Governor
of Quebec, Montmagny, saw a rival governor in Maisonneuve. Every means was used to persuade the advent-
urers to abandon their project, and settle at Quebec.
Montmagny called a council of the principal persons of
his colony, who gave it as their opinion that the new-
comers had better exchange Montreal for the Island of
Orleans, where they would be in a position to give and
receive succor; while, by persisting in their first design,
they would expose themselves to destruction, and be of
use to nobody. Maisonneuve, who was present, expressed
his surprise that they should assume to direct his affairs.
"I have not come here," he said, "to deliberate, but
to act. It is my duty and my honor to found a colony at Montreal; and I would go, if every tree were an
Iroquois!"

At Quebec there was little ability and no inclination
to shelter the new colonists for the winter; and they
would have fared ill, but for the generosity of M. Pui-
seaux, who lived not far distant, at a place called St.
Michel. This devout and most hospitable person made
room for them all in his rough, but capacious dwelling.
Their neighbors were the hospital nuns, then living at

the mission of Sillery, in a substantial, but comfortless house of stone; where, amidst destitution, sickness, and irrepressible disgust at the filth of the savages whom they had in charge, they were laboring day and night with devoted assiduity. Among the minor ills which beset them were the eccentricities of one of their lay sisters, crazed with religious enthusiasm, who had the care of their poultry and domestic animals, of which she was accustomed to inquire, one by one, if they loved God; when, not receiving an immediate answer in the affirmative, she would instantly put them to death, telling them that their impiety deserved no better fate.

Early in May, Maisonneuve and his followers embarked. They had gained an unexpected recruit during the winter, in the person of Madame de la Peltrie, foundress of the Ursulines of Quebec. The piety, the novelty, and the romance of their enterprise, all had their charms for the fair enthusiast; and an irresistible impulse — imputed by a slandering historian to the levity of her sex — urged her to share their fortunes. Her zeal was more admired by the Montrealists whom she joined than by the Ursulines whom she abandoned. She carried off all the furniture she had lent them, and left them in the utmost destitution. Nor did she remain quiet after reaching Montreal, but was presently seized with a longing to visit the Hurons, and preach the Faith in person to those benighted heathen. It needed all the eloquence of a Jesuit, lately returned from that most arduous mission, to convince her that the attempt would be as useless as rash.

It was the eighth of May when Maisonneuve and his followers embarked at St. Michel; and as the boats, deep-laden with men, arms, and stores, moved slowly on their way, the forest, with leaves just opening in the warmth of spring, lay on their right hand and on their left, in a flattering semblance of tranquillity and peace. But behind woody islets, in tangled thickets and damp ravines, and in the shade and stillness of the columned woods, lurked everywhere a danger and a terror.

On the seventeenth of May, 1642, Maisonneuve's little flotilla — a pinnace, a flat-bottomed craft moved by sails, and two row-boats — approached Montreal; and all on board raised in unison a hymn of praise. Montmagny was with them, to deliver the island, in behalf of the Company of the Hundred Associates, to Maisonneuve, representative of the Associates of Montreal. And here, too, was Father Vimont, Superior of the missions; for the Jesuits had been prudently invited to accept the spiritual charge of the young colony. On the following day, they glided along the green and solitary shores now thronged with the life of a busy city, and landed on the spot which Champlain, thirty-one years before, had chosen as the fit site of a settlement. It was a tongue or triangle of land, formed by the junction of a rivulet with the St. Lawrence, and known afterwards as Point Callière. The rivulet was bordered by a meadow, and beyond rose the forest with its vanguard of scattered trees. Early spring flowers were blooming in the young grass, and birds of varied plumage flitted among the boughs.

Maisonneuve sprang ashore, and fell on his knees. His followers imitated his example; and all joined their voices in enthusiastic songs of thanksgiving. Tents, baggage, arms, and stores were landed. An altar was raised on a pleasant spot near at hand; and Mademoiselle Mance, with Madame de la Peltrie, aided by her servant, Charlotte Barré, decorated it with a taste which was the admiration of the beholders. Now all the company gathered before the shrine. Here stood Vimont, in the rich vestments of his office. Here were the two ladies, with their servant; Montmagny, no very willing spectator; and Maisonneuve, a warlike figure, erect and tall, his men clustering around him, — soldiers, sailors, artisans, and laborers, — all alike soldiers at need. They knelt in reverent silence as the Host was raised aloft; and when the rite was over, the priest turned and addressed them : —

" You are a grain of mustard-seed, that shall rise and grow till its branches overshadow the earth. You are few, but your work is the work of God. His smile is on you, and your children shall fill the land."

The afternoon waned; the sun sank behind the western forest, and twilight came on. Fireflies were twinkling over the darkened meadow. They caught them, tied them with threads into shining festoons, and hung them before the altar, where the Host remained exposed. Then they pitched their tents, lighted their bivouac fires, stationed their guards, and lay down to rest. Such was the birth-night of Montreal.

Is this true history, or a romance of Christian chivalry? It is both.

A few years later there was another emigration to Montreal, of a character much like the first. The pious little colony led a struggling and precarious existence. Many of its inhabitants were killed by the Iroquois, and its escape from destruction was imputed to the intervention of the Holy Virgin. The place changed as years went on, and became a great centre of the fur trade, though still bearing strong marks of its pristine character. The institutions of religion and charity planted by its founders remain to this day, and the Seminary

of St. Sulpice holds vast possessions in and around
the city.   During the war of 1755–1760, Montreal
was a base of military operations.   In the latter year
three English armies advanced upon it from three
different points, united before its walls, and forced
Governor Vaudreuil to surrender all Canada to the
British Crown.

QUEBEC.

CHAMPLAIN was the founder of this old capital of French Canada, whose existence began in 1608. In that year he built a cluster of fortified dwellings and storehouses, which he called "The Habitation of Quebec," and which stood on or near the site of the market-place of the Lower Town.

The settlement made little progress for many years. A company of merchants held the monopoly of its fur-trade, by which alone it lived. It was half trading-factory, half mission. Its permanent inmates did not exceed fifty or sixty persons, — fur-traders, friars, and two or three wretched families, who had no inducement and little wish to labor. The fort is facetiously represented as having two old women for garrison, and a brace of hens for sentinels. All was discord and disorder. Champlain was the nominal commander; but the actual authority was with the merchants, who held, excepting the friars, nearly every one in their pay. Each was jealous of the other, but all were united in a common jealousy of Champlain. From a short-sighted view of self-interest, they sought to check the colonization which they were pledged to promote. The few families whom they brought over were forbidden to trade with the Indians, and compelled to sell the fruits of their labor to the agents of the company at a low, fixed price, receiving goods in return at an inordinate

valuation. Some of the merchants were of Rouen, some
of St. Malo; some were Catholics, some were Huguenots.
Hence unceasing bickerings. All exercise of the Re-
formed Religion, on land or water, was prohibited within
the limits of New France; but the Huguenots set the
prohibition at nought, roaring their heretical psalmody
with such vigor from their ships in the river, that the
unhallowed strains polluted the ears of the Indians on
shore. The merchants of Rochelle, who had refused to
join the company, carried on a bold, illicit traffic along
the borders of the St. Lawrence, eluding pursuit, or, if
hard pressed, showing fight; and this was a source of
perpetual irritation to the incensed monopolists.

Champlain, in his singularly trying position, displayed
a mingled zeal and fortitude. He went every year to
France, laboring for the interests of the colony. To
throw open the trade to all competitors was a measure
beyond the wisdom of the times; and he aimed only so
to bind and regulate the monopoly as to make it sub-
serve the generous purpose to which he had given himself. He had succeeded in binding the company of
merchants with new and more stringent engagements;
and, in the vain belief that these might not be wholly
broken, he began to conceive fresh hopes for the colony.
In this faith he embarked with his wife for Quebec in
the spring of 1620; and, as the boat drew near the
landing, the cannon welcomed her to the rock of her
banishment. The buildings were falling to ruin; rain
entered on all sides; the court-yard, says Champlain,
was as squalid and dilapidated as a grange pillaged by
soldiers. Madame de Champlain was still very young.
If the Ursuline tradition is to be trusted, the Indians,
amazed at her beauty and touched by her gentleness,
would have worshipped her as a divinity. Her husband

had married her at the age of twelve; when, to his horror, he presently discovered that she was infected with the heresies of her father, a disguised Huguenot. He addressed himself at once to her conversion, and his pious efforts were something more than successful. During the four years which she passed in Canada, her zeal, it is true, was chiefly exercised in admonishing Indian squaws and catechising their children; but, on her return to France, nothing would content her but to become a nun. Champlain refused; but, as she was childless, he at length consented to a virtual, though not formal, separation. After his death she gained her wish, became an Ursuline nun, founded a convent of that order at Meaux, and died with a reputation almost saintly.

A stranger visiting the fort of Quebec would have been astonished at its air of conventual decorum. Black Jesuits and scarfed officers mingled at Champlain's table. There was little conversation, but, in its place, histories and the lives of saints were read aloud, as in a monastic refectory. Prayers, masses, and confessions followed each other with an edifying regularity, and the bell of the adjacent chapel, built by Champlain, rang morning, noon, and night. Godless soldiers caught the infection, and whipped themselves in penance for their sins. Debauched artisans outdid each other in the fury of their contrition. Quebec was become a Mission. Indians gathered thither as of old, not from the baneful lure of brandy, for the traffic in it was no longer tolerated, but from the less pernicious attractions of gifts, kind words, and politic blandishments. To the vital principle of propagandism the commercial and the military character were subordinated; or, to speak more justly, trade, policy, and military power leaned on the missions as their main support, the grand instrument of their extension. The missions were to explore the interior; the missions were to win over the savage hordes at once to Heaven and to France.

Years passed. The mission of the Hurons was established, and here the indomitable Brébeuf, with a band worthy of him, toiled amid miseries and perils as fearful as ever shook the constancy of man; while Champlain at Quebec, in a life uneventful, yet harassing and laborious, was busied in the round of cares which his post involved.

Christmas day, 1635, was a dark day in the annals of New France. In a chamber of the fort, breathless and cold, lay the hardy frame which war, the wilderness, and the sea had buffeted so long in vain. After two months and a half of illness, Champlain, at the age of sixty-eight, was dead. His last cares were for his colony and the succor of its suffering families. Jesuits, officers, soldiers, traders, and the few settlers of Quebec followed his remains to the church; Le Jeune pronounced his eulogy, and the feeble community built a tomb to his honor.

The colony could ill spare him. For twenty-seven years he had labored hard and ceaselessly for its welfare, sacrificing fortune, repose, and domestic peace to a cause embraced with enthusiasm and pursued with intrepid persistency. His character belonged partly to the past, partly to the present. The *preux chevalier*, the crusader, the romance-loving explorer, the curious, knowledge-seeking traveller, the practical navigator, all claimed their share in him. His views, though far beyond those of the mean spirits around him, belonged to his age and his creed. He was less statesman than soldier. He leaned to the most direct and boldest policy, and one of his last acts was to petition Richelieu for men and munitions for repressing that standing menace to the colony, the Iroquois. His dauntless courage was matched by an unwearied patience, a patience proved by life-long vexations, and not wholly subdued even by the saintly follies of his wife. He is charged with credulity, from which few of his age were free, and which in all ages has been the foible of earnest and generous natures, too ardent to criticise, and too honorable to doubt the honor of others. Perhaps in his later years the heretic might like him more had the Jesuit liked him less. The adventurous explorer of Lake Huron, the bold invader of the Iroquois, befits but indifferently the monastic sobrieties of the fort of Quebec and his sombre environment of priests. Yet Champlain was no formalist, nor was his an empty zeal. A soldier from his youth, in an age of unbridled license, his life had answered to his maxims; and when a generation had passed after his visit to the Hurons, their elders remembered with astonishment the continence of the great French war-chief.

His books mark the man, — all for his theme and his purpose, nothing for himself. Crude in style, full of the superficial errors of carelessness and haste, rarely diffuse, often brief to a fault, they bear on every page the palpable impress of truth.

QUEBEC was without a governor. Who should succeed Champlain? and would his successor be found equally zealous for the Faith, and friendly to the mission? These doubts, as he himself tells us, agitated the mind of the Father Superior, Le Jeune; but they were happily set at rest, when, on a morning in June, he saw a ship anchoring in the basin below, and, hastening with his brethren to the landing-place, was there met by Charles Huault de Montmagny, a Knight of Malta, followed by a train of officers and gentlemen. As they all climbed the rock together, Montmagny saw a crucifix planted by the path. He instantly fell on his knees before it; and nobles, soldiers, sailors, and priests imitated his example. The Jesuits sang Te Deum at the church, and the cannon roared from the adjacent fort. Here the new governor was scarcely installed, when a Jesuit came in to ask if he would be godfather to an Indian about to be baptized. "Most gladly," replied the pious Montmagny. He repaired on the instant to the convert's hut, with a company of gayly apparelled gentlemen; and while the inmates stared in amazement at the scarlet and embroidery, he bestowed on the dying savage the name of Joseph, in honor of the spouse of the Virgin and the patron of New France. Three days after, he was told that a dead proselyte was to be buried, on which, leaving the lines

of the new fortification he was tracing, he took in hand
a torch, De Lisle, his lieutenant, took another, Repentigny and St. Jean, gentlemen of his suite, with a band
of soldiers, followed, two priests bore the corpse, and
thus all moved together in procession to the place of
burial. The Jesuits were comforted. Champlain himself had not displayed a zeal so edifying.

A considerable reinforcement came out with Montmagny, and among the rest several men of birth and
substance, with their families and dependants. "It was
a sight to thank God for," exclaims Father Le Jeune,
"to behold these delicate young ladies and these tender
infants issuing from their wooden prison, like day from
the shades of night." The Father, it will be remembered,
had for some years past seen nothing but squaws, with
pappooses swathed like mummies and strapped to a
board.

Both Montmagny and De Lisle were half churchmen,
for both were Knights of Malta. More and more the
powers spiritual engrossed the colony. As nearly as
might be, the sword itself was in priestly hands. The
Jesuits were all in all. Authority, absolute and without
appeal, was vested in a council composed of the governor,
Le Jeune, and the syndic, an official supposed to represent the interests of the inhabitants. There was no
tribunal of justice, and the governor pronounced sum-
marily on all complaints. The church adjoined the
fort; and before it was planted a stake bearing a placard
with a prohibition against blasphemy, drunkenness, or
neglect of mass and other religious rites. To the stake
was also attached a chain and iron collar; and hard by
was a wooden horse, whereon a culprit was now and
then mounted by way of example and warning. In a
community so absolutely priest-governed, overt offences
9

were, however, rare; and, except on the annual arrival
of the ships from France, when the rock swarmed with
godless sailors, Quebec was a model of decorum, and
wore, as its chroniclers tell us, an aspect unspeakably
edifying.

In the year 1640, various new establishments of
religion and charity might have been seen at Quebec.
There was the beginning of a college and a seminary
for Huron children, an embryo Ursuline convent, an
incipient hospital, and a new Algonquin mission at a
place called Sillery, four miles distant. Champlain's
fort had been enlarged and partly rebuilt in stone by
Montmagny, who had also laid out streets on the site of
the future city, though as yet the streets had no houses.
Behind the fort, and very near it, stood the church and
a house for the Jesuits. Both were of pine wood; and
this year, 1640, both were burned to the ground, to be
afterwards rebuilt in stone.

Aside from the fur trade of the Company, the whole
life of the colony was in missions, convents, religious
schools, and hospitals. Here on the rock of Quebec
were the appendages, useful and otherwise, of an old-
established civilization. While as yet there were no
inhabitants, and no immediate hope of any, there were
institutions for the care of children, the sick, and the
decrepit. All these were supported by a charity in
most cases precarious. The Jesuits relied chiefly on
the Company, who, by the terms of their patent, were
obliged to maintain religious worship.

Quebec wore an aspect half military, half monastic.
At sunrise and sunset, a squad of soldiers in the pay of
the Company paraded in the fort; and, as in Champlain's
time, the bells of the church rang morning, noon, and
night. Confessions, masses, and penances were punc-

tiliously observed ; and, from the governor to the mean-
est laborer, the Jesuit watched and guided all. The
social atmosphere of New England itself was not more
suffocating. By day and by night, at home, at church,
or at his daily work, the colonist lived under the eyes
of busy and over-zealous priests. At times, the denizens
of Quebec grew restless. In 1639, deputies were covertly
sent to beg relief in France, and " to represent the hell
in which the consciences of the colony were kept by the
union of the temporal and spiritual authority in the
same hands."

The very amusements of this pious community were
acts of religion. Thus, on the fête-day of St. Joseph,
the patron of New France, there was a show of fireworks
to do him honor. In the forty volumes of the Jesuit
Relations there is but one pictorial illustration ; and
this represents the pyrotechnic contrivance in question,
together with a figure of the Governor in the act of
touching it off. But, what is more curious, a Catholic
writer of the present day, the Abbé Faillon, in an elabo-
rate and learned work, dilates at length on the details
of the display ; and this, too, with a gravity which
evinces his conviction that squibs, rockets, blue-lights,
and serpents are important instruments for the saving
of souls. On May-Day of the same year, 1637, Montmagny planted before the church a May-pole surmounted
by a triple crown, beneath which were three symbolical
circles decorated with wreaths, and bearing severally
the names, *Iesus, Maria, Ioseph ;* the soldiers drew up
before it, and saluted it with a volley of musketry.

On the anniversary of the Dauphin's birth there was
a dramatic performance, in which an unbeliever, speaking
Algonquin for the profit of the Indians present, was
hunted into Hell by fiends. Religious processions were

frequent. In one of them, the Governor in a court dress and a baptized Indian in beaver-skins were joint supporters of the canopy which covered the Host. In another, six Indians led the van, arrayed each in a velvet coat of scarlet and gold sent them by the King. Then came other Indian converts, two and two; then the foundress of the Ursuline convent, with Indian children in French gowns; then all the Indian girls and women, dressed after their own way; then the priests; then the Governor; and finally the whole French population, male and female, except the artillery-men at the fort, who saluted with their cannon the cross and banner borne at the head of the procession. When all was over, the Governor and the Jesuits rewarded the Indians with a feast.

Now let the stranger enter the church of Notre-Dame de la Recouvrance, after vespers. It is full, to the very porch: officers in slouched hats and plumes, musketeers, pikemen, mechanics, and laborers. Here is Montmagny himself; Repentigny and Poterie, gentlemen of good birth; damsels of nurture ill fitted to the Canadian woods; and, mingled with these, the motionless Indians, wrapped to the throat in embroidered moose-hides. Le Jeune, not in priestly vestments, but in the common black dress of his Order, is before the altar; and on either side is a row of small red-skinned children listening with exemplary decorum, while, with a cheerful, smiling face, he teaches them to kneel, clasp their hands, and sign the cross. All the principal members of this zealous community are present, at once amused and edified at the grave deportment, and the prompt, shrill replies of the infant catechumens; while their parents in the crowd grin delight at the gifts of beads and trinkets with which Le Jeune rewards his most proficient pupils.

The methods of conversion were simple. The principal appeal was to fear. "You do good to your friends," said Le Jeune to an Algonquin chief, "and you burn your enemies. God does the same." And he painted Hell to the startled neophyte as a place where, when he was hungry, he would get nothing to eat but frogs and snakes, and, when thirsty, nothing to drink but flames. Pictures were found invaluable. "These holy representations," pursues the Father Superior, "are half the instruction that can be given to the Indians. I wanted some pictures of Hell and souls in perdition, and a few were sent us on paper; but they are too confused. The devils and the men are so mixed up, that one can make out nothing without particular attention. If three, four, or five devils were painted tormenting a soul with different punishments, — one applying fire, another serpents, another tearing him with pincers, and another holding him fast with a chain, — this would have a good effect, especially if everything were made distinct, and misery, rage, and desperation appeared plainly in his face."

The preparation of the convert for baptism was often very slight. A dying Algonquin, who, though meagre as a skeleton, had thrown himself, with a last effort of expiring ferocity, on an Iroquois prisoner, and torn off his ear with his teeth, was baptized almost immediately. In the case of converts in health there was far more preparation; yet these often apostatized. The various objects of instruction may all be included in one comprehensive word, submission, — an abdication of will and judgment in favor of the spiritual director, who was the interpreter and vicegerent of God.

LIKE Montreal, Quebec transformed itself in time lost much of its character of a mission, and became the seat of the colonial government. In short, it became secularized, though not completely so; for the priesthood still held an immense influence and disputed the mastery with the civil and military powers.

In the beginning of William and Mary's War, Count Frontenac, governor of Canada, sent repeated war-parties to harass the New England borders; and, in 1690, the General Court of Massachusetts resolved to retort by a decisive blow. Sir William Phips was chosen to command the intended expedition. Phips is said to have been one of twenty-six children, all of the same mother, and was born in 1650 at a rude border settlement, since called Woolwich, on the Kennebec. His parents were ignorant and poor; and till eighteen years of age he was employed in keeping sheep. Such a life ill suited his active and ambitious nature. To better his condition, he learned the trade of ship-carpenter, and, in the exercise of it, came to Boston, where he married a widow with some property, beyond him in years, and much above him in station. About this time, he learned to read and write, though not too well, for his signature is like that of a peasant. Still aspiring to greater things, he promised his wife that he would one day command a king's ship and own a " fair brick house

in the Green Lane of North Boston," a quarter then
occupied by citizens of the better class. He kept his
word at both points. Fortune was inauspicious to him
for several years; till at length, under the pressure of
reverses, he conceived the idea of conquering fame and
wealth at one stroke, by fishing up the treasure said to
be stored in a Spanish galleon wrecked fifty years before
somewhere in the West Indian seas. Full of this project, he went to England, where, through influences
which do not plainly appear, he gained a hearing from
persons in high places, and induced the Admiralty to
adopt his scheme. A frigate was given him, and he
sailed for the West Indies; whence, after a long search,
he returned unsuccessful, though not without adventures
which proved his mettle. It was the epoch of the buc-
caneers; and his crew, tired of a vain and toilsome
search, came to the quarter-deck, armed with cutlasses,
and demanded of their captain that he should turn pirate
with them. Phips, a tall and powerful man, instantly
fell upon them with his fists, knocked down the ring-
leaders, and awed them all into submission. Not long
after, there was a more formidable mutiny; but, with
great courage and address, he quelled it for a time, and
held his crew to their duty till he had brought the ship
into Jamaica, and exchanged them for better men.

Though the leaky condition of the frigate compelled
him to abandon the search, it was not till he had gained
information which he thought would lead to success;
and, on his return, he inspired such confidence that the
Duke of Albemarle, with other noblemen and gentlemen,
gave him a fresh outfit, and despatched him again on
his Quixotic errand. This time he succeeded, found the
wreck, and took from it gold, silver, and jewels to the
value of three hundred thousand pounds sterling. The

crew now leagued together to seize the ship and divide the prize; and Phips, pushed to extremity, was compelled to promise that every man of them should have a share in the treasure, even if he paid it himself. On reaching England, he kept his pledge so well that, after redeeming it, only sixteen thousand pounds was left as his portion, which, however, was an ample fortune in the New England of that day. He gained, too, what he valued almost as much, the honor of knighthood. Tempting offers were made him of employment in the royal service; but he had an ardent love for his own country, and thither he presently returned.

Phips was a rude sailor, bluff, prompt, and choleric. He never gave proof of intellectual capacity; and such of his success in life as he did not owe to good luck was due probably to an energetic and adventurous spirit, aided by a blunt frankness of address that pleased the great, and commended him to their favor. Two years after the expedition against Quebec, the king, under the new charter, made him governor of Massachusetts, a post for which, though totally unfit, he had been recommended by the elder Mather, who, like his son Cotton, expected to make use of him. He carried his old habits into his new office, cudgelled Brinton, the collector of the port, and belabored Captain Short of the royal navy with his cane. Far from trying to hide the obscurity of his origin, he leaned to the opposite foible, and was apt to boast of it, delighting to exhibit himself as a self-made man. New England writers describe him as honest in private dealings; but, in accordance with his coarse nature, he seems to have thought that anything is fair in war. On the other hand, he was warmly patriotic, and was almost as ready to serve New England as to serve himself.

Returning from an expedition to Acadia, he found Boston alive with martial preparation. Massachusetts of her own motion had resolved to attempt the conquest of Quebec. She and her sister colonies had not yet recovered from the exhaustion of Philip's War, and still less from the disorders that attended the expulsion of the royal governor and his adherents. The public treasury was empty, and the recent expeditions against the eastern Indians had been supported by private subscription. Worse yet, New England had no competent military commander. The Puritan gentlemen of the original emigration, some of whom were as well fitted for military as for civil leadership, had passed from the stage; and, by a tendency which circumstances made inevitable, they had left none behind them equally qualified. The great Indian conflict of fifteen years before had, it is true, formed good partisan chiefs, and proved that the New England yeoman, defending his family and his hearth, was not to be surpassed in stubborn fighting; but, since Andros and his soldiers had been driven out, there was scarcely a single man in the colony of the slightest training or experience in regular war. Up to this moment, New England had never asked help of the mother country. When thousands of savages burst on her defenceless settlements, she had conquered safety and peace with her own blood and her own slender resources; but now, as the proposed capture of Quebec would inure to the profit of the British crown, Governor Bradstreet and his council thought it not unfitting to ask for a supply of arms and ammunition, of which they were in great need. The request was refused, and no aid of any kind came from the English government, whose resources were engrossed by the Irish war.

While waiting for the reply, the colonial authorities

urged on their preparations, in the hope that the plunder of Quebec would pay the expenses of its conquest. Humility was not among the New England virtues, and it was thought a sin to doubt that God would give his chosen people the victory over papists and idolaters; yet no pains were spared to insure the divine favor. A proclamation was issued, calling the people to repentance; a day of fasting was ordained; and, as Mather expresses it, "the wheel of prayer was kept in continual motion." The chief difficulty was to provide funds. An attempt was made to collect a part of the money by private subscription; but, as this plan failed, the provisional government, already in debt, strained its credit yet farther, and borrowed the needful sums. Thirty-two trading and fishing vessels, great and small, were impressed for the service. The largest was a ship called the "Six Friends," engaged in the dangerous West India trade, and carrying forty-four guns. A call was made for volunteers, and many enrolled themselves; but, as more were wanted, a press was ordered to complete the number. So rigorously was it applied that, what with voluntary and enforced enlistment, one town, that of Gloucester, was deprived of two thirds of its fencible men. There was not a moment of doubt as to the choice of a commander, for Phips was imagined to be the very man for the work. One John Walley, a respectable citizen of Barnstable, was made second in command, with the modest rank of major; and a sufficient number of ship-masters, merchants, master mechanics, and substantial farmers, were commissioned as subordinate officers. About the middle of July, the committee charged with the preparations reported that all was ready. Still there was a long delay. The vessel sent early in spring to ask aid from England had

not returned. Phips waited for her as long as he dared,
and the best of the season was over when he resolved
to put to sea. The rustic warriors, duly formed into
companies, were sent on board; and the fleet sailed
from Nantasket on the ninth of August. Including
sailors, it carried twenty-two hundred men, with provisions for four months, but insufficient ammunition and
no pilot for the St. Lawrence.

The delay at Boston, waiting aid from England that
never came, was not propitious to Phips; nor were the
wind and the waves. The voyage to the St. Lawrence
was a long one; and when he began, without a pilot, to
grope his way up the unknown river, the weather seemed
in league with his enemies. He appears, moreover, to
have wasted time. What was most vital to his success
was rapidity of movement; yet, whether by his fault or
his misfortune, he remained three weeks within three
days' sail of Quebec. While anchored off Tadoussac,
with the wind ahead, he passed the idle hours in holding
councils of war and framing rules for the government
of his men; and, when at length the wind veered to
the east, it is doubtful if he made the best use of his
opportunity.

When, after his protracted voyage, Phips sailed into
the Basin of Quebec, one of the grandest scenes on the
western continent opened upon his sight: the wide expanse of waters, the lofty promontory beyond, and the
opposing heights of Levi; the cataract of Montmorenci,
the distant range of the Laurentian Mountains, the warlike rock with its diadem of walls and towers, the roofs
of the Lower Town clustering on the strand beneath,
the Château St. Louis perched at the brink of the cliff,
and over it the white banner, spangled with *fleurs-de-lis*,
flaunting defiance in the clear autumnal air. Perhaps,

as he gazed, a suspicion seized him that the task he had undertaken was less easy than he had thought; but he had conquered once by a simple summons to surrender, and he resolved to try its virtue again.

The fleet anchored a little below Quebec; and towards ten o'clock the French saw a boat put out from the admiral's ship, bearing a flag of truce. Four canoes went from the Lower Town, and met it midway. It brought a subaltern officer, who announced himself as the bearer of a letter from Sir William Phips to the French commander. He was taken into one of the canoes and paddled to the quay, after being completely blindfolded by a bandage which covered half his face. An officer named Prévost, sent by Count Frontenac, received him as he landed, and ordered two sergeants to take him by the arms and lead him to the governor. His progress was neither rapid nor direct. They drew him hither and thither, delighting to make him clamber in the dark over every possible obstruction; while a noisy crowd hustled him, and laughing women called him Colin Maillard, the name of the chief player in blindman's buff. Amid a prodigious hubbub, intended to bewilder him and impress him with a sense of immense warlike preparation, they dragged him over the three barricades of Mountain Street, and brought him at last into a large room of the château. Here they took the bandage from his eyes. He stood for a moment with an air of astonishment and some confusion. The governor stood before him, haughty and stern, surrounded by French and Canadian officers, Maricourt, Sainte-Hélène, Longueuil, Villebon, Valrenne, Bienville, and many more, bedecked with gold lace and silver lace, perukes and powder, plumes and ribbons, and all the martial foppery in which they took delight, and regarding the envoy with keen, defiant eyes. After a moment, he recovered his breath and his composure, saluted Frontenac, and, expressing a wish that the duty assigned him had been of a more agreeable nature, handed him the letter of Phips. Frontenac gave it to an interpreter, who read it aloud in French that all might hear. It ran thus : —

" *Sir William Phips, Knight, General and Commander-in-chief in and over their Majesties' Forces of New England, by Sea and Land, to Count Frontenac, Lieutenant-General and Governour for the French King at Canada ; or, in his absence, to his Deputy, or him or them in chief command at Quebeck :*

" The war between the crowns of England and France doth not only sufficiently warrant, but the destruction made by the French and Indians, under your command and encouragement, upon the persons and estates of their Majesties' subjects of New England, without provocation on their part, hath put them under the necessity of this expedition for their own security and satisfaction. And although the cruelties and barbarities used against them by the French and Indians might, upon the present opportunity, prompt unto a severe revenge, yet, being desirous to avoid all inhumane and unchristian-like actions, and to prevent shedding of blood as much as may be,

" I, the aforesaid William Phips, Knight, do hereby, in the name and in the behalf of their most excellent Majesties, William and Mary, King and Queen of England, Scotland, France, and Ireland, Defenders of the Faith, and by order of their said Majesties' government of the Massachuset-colony in New England, demand a present surrender of your forts and castles, undemolished, and the King's and other stores, unimbezzled, with a seasonable delivery of all captives ; together with a surrender of all your persons and estates to my dispose : upon the doing whereof, you may expect mercy from me, as a Christian, according to what shall be found for their Majesties' service and the subjects' security. Which, if you refuse forthwith to do, I am come provided, and am resolved, by the help of God, in whom I trust, by force of arms to revenge all wrongs and injuries offered, and bring you under subjection to the Crown of England, and, when too late, make you wish you had accepted of the favour tendered.

"Your answer positive in an hour, returned by your own trumpet, with the return of mine, is required upon the peril that will ensue."

When the reading was finished, the Englishman pulled his watch from his pocket, and handed it to the governor. Frontenac could not, or pretended that he could not, see the hour. The messenger thereupon told him that it was ten o'clock, and that he must have his answer before eleven. A general cry of indignation arose; and Valrenne called out that Phips was nothing but a pirate, and that his man ought to be hanged. Frontenac contained himself for a moment, and then said to the envoy : —

"I will not keep you waiting so long. Tell your general that I do not recognize King William ; and that the Prince of Orange, who so styles himself, is a usurper, who has violated the most sacred laws of blood in attempting to dethrone his father-in-law. I know no king of England but King James. Your general ought not to be surprised at the hostilities which he says that the French have carried on in the colony of Massachusetts ; for, as the king my master has taken the king of England under his protection, and is about to replace him on his throne by force of arms, he might have expected that his Majesty would order me to make war on a people who have rebelled against their lawful prince." Then, turning with a smile to the officers about him : "Even if your general offered me conditions a little more gracious, and if I had a mind to accept them, does he suppose that these brave gentlemen would give their consent, and advise me to trust a man who broke his agreement with the governor of Port Royal, or a rebel who has failed in his duty to his king, and forgotten all the favors he had received from him, to follow a prince who pretends to be the liberator of England and the defender of the faith, and yet destroys the laws and privileges of the kingdom and overthrows its religion? The divine justice which your general invokes in his letter will not fail to punish such acts severely."

The messenger seemed astonished and startled; but he presently asked if the governor would give him his answer in writing.

"No," returned Frontenac, "I will answer your general only by the mouths of my cannon, that he may learn that a man like me is not to be summoned after this fashion. Let him do his best, and I will do mine;" and he dismissed the Englishman abruptly. He was again blindfolded, led over the barricades, and sent back to the fleet by the boat that brought him.

Phips had often given proof of personal courage, but for the past three weeks his conduct seems that of a man conscious that he is charged with a work too large for his capacity. He had spent a good part of his time in holding councils of war; and now, when he heard the answer of Frontenac, he called another to consider what should be done. A plan of attack was at length arranged. The militia were to be landed on the shore of Beauport, which was just below Quebec, though separated from it by the St. Charles. They were then to cross this river by a ford practicable at low water, climb the heights of St. Geneviève, and gain the rear of the town. The small vessels of the fleet were to aid the movement by ascending the St. Charles as far as the ford, holding the enemy in check by their fire, and carrying provisions, ammunition, and intrenching tools, for the use of the land troops. When these had crossed and were ready to attack Quebec in the rear, Phips was to cannonade it in front, and land two hundred men under cover of his guns to effect a diversion by storming the barricades. Some of the French prisoners, from whom their captors appear to have received a great deal of correct information, told the admiral that there was a place a mile or two above the town where the heights might be scaled and the rear of the fortifications reached from a direction opposite to that proposed. This was precisely the movement by which Wolfe afterwards gained his memorable victory; but Phips chose to abide by the original plan.

While the plan was debated, the opportunity for accomplishing it ebbed away. It was still early when the messenger returned from Quebec; but, before Phips was ready to act, the day was on the wane and the tide was against him. He lay quietly at his moorings when, in the evening, a great shouting, mingled with the roll of drums and the sound of fifes, was heard from the Upper Town. The English officers asked their prisoner, Granville, what it meant. "Ma foi, Messieurs," he replied, "you have lost the game. It is the Governor of Montreal with the people from the country above. There is nothing for you now but to pack and go home." In fact, Callières had arrived with seven or eight hundred men, many of them regulars. With these were bands of *coureurs de bois* and other young Canadians, all full of fight, singing and whooping with martial glee as they passed the western gate and trooped down St. Louis Street.

The next day was gusty and blustering; and still Phips

lay quiet, waiting on the winds and the waves. A small vessel, with sixty men on board, under Captain Ephraim Savage, ran in towards the shore of Beauport to examine the landing, and stuck fast in the mud. The Canadians plied her with bullets, and brought a cannon to bear on her. They might have waded out and boarded her, but Savage and his men kept up so hot a fire that they forbore the attempt; and, when the tide rose, she floated again.

There was another night of tranquillity; but at about eleven on Wednesday morning the French heard the English fifes and drums in full action, while repeated shouts of "God save King William!" rose from all the vessels. This lasted an hour or more; after which a great number of boats, loaded with men, put out from the fleet and rowed rapidly towards the shore of Beauport. The tide was low, and the boats grounded before reaching the landing-place. The French on the rock could see the troops through telescopes, looking in the distance like a swarm of black ants, as they waded through mud and water, and formed in companies along the strand. They were some thirteen hundred in number, and were commanded by Major Walley. Frontenac had sent three hundred sharpshooters, under Sainte-Hélène, to meet them and hold them in check. A battalion of troops followed; but, long before they could reach the spot, Sainte-Hélène's men, with a few militia from the neighboring parishes, and a band of Huron warriors from Lorette, threw themselves into the thickets along the front of the English, and opened a distant but galling fire upon the compact bodies of the enemy. Walley ordered a charge. The New England men rushed, in a disorderly manner, but with great impetuosity, up the rising ground; received two volleys, which failed to

10

check them; and drove back the assailants in some confusion. They turned, however, and fought in Indian fashion with courage and address, leaping and dodging among trees, rocks, and bushes, firing as they retreated, and inflicting more harm than they received. Towards evening they disappeared; and Walley, whose men had been much scattered in the desultory fight, drew them together as well as he could, and advanced towards the St. Charles, in order to meet the vessels which were to aid him in passing the ford. Here he posted sentinels, and encamped for the night. He had lost four killed and about sixty wounded, and imagined that he had killed twenty or thirty of the enemy. In fact, however, their loss was much less, though among the killed was a valuable officer, the Chevalier de Clermont, and among the wounded the veteran captain of Beauport, Juchereau de Saint-Denis, more than sixty-four years of age. In the evening, a deserter came to the English camp, and brought the unwelcome intelligence that there were three thousand armed men in Quebec.

Meanwhile, Phips, whose fault hitherto had not been an excess of promptitude, grew impatient, and made a premature movement inconsistent with the preconcerted plan. He left his moorings, anchored his largest ships before the town, and prepared to cannonade it; but the fiery veteran who watched him from the Château St. Louis anticipated him, and gave him the first shot. Phips replied furiously, opening fire with every gun that he could bring to bear; while the rock paid him back in kind, and belched flame and smoke from all its batteries. So fierce and rapid was the firing, that La Hontan compares it to volleys of musketry; and old officers, who had seen many sieges, declared that they had never known the like. The din was prodigious, reverberated from the surrounding heights, and rolled back from the distant mountains in one continuous roar. On the part of the English, however, surprisingly little was accomplished beside noise and smoke. The practice of their gunners was so bad that many of their shot struck harmlessly against the face of the cliff. Their guns, too, were very light, and appear to have been charged with a view to the most rigid economy of gunpowder: for the balls failed to pierce the stone walls of the buildings, and did so little damage that, as the French boasted, twenty crowns would have repaired it all. Night came at length, and the turmoil ceased.

Phips lay quiet till daybreak, when Frontenac sent a shot to waken him, and the cannonade began again. Sainte-Hélène had returned from Beauport; and he, with his brother Maricourt, took charge of the two batteries of the Lower Town, aiming the guns in person, and throwing balls of eighteen and twenty-four pounds with excellent precision against the four largest ships of the fleet. One of their shots cut the flagstaff of the admiral, and the cross of St. George fell into the river. It drifted with the tide towards the north shore; whereupon several Canadians paddled out in a birch canoe, secured it, and brought it back in triumph. On the spire of the cathedral in the Upper Town had been hung a picture of the Holy Family, as an invocation of divine aid. The Puritan gunners wasted their ammunition in vain attempts to knock it down. That it escaped their malice was ascribed to miracle, but the miracle would have been greater if they had hit it.

At length, one of the ships, which had suffered most, hauled off and abandoned the fight. That of the admiral had fared little better, and now her condition grew desperate. With her rigging torn, her mainmast half cut through, her mizzen-mast splintered, her cabin pierced, and her hull riddled with shot, another volley seemed likely to sink her, when Phips ordered her to be cut loose from her moorings, and she drifted out of fire, leaving cable and anchor behind. The remaining ships soon gave over the conflict, and withdrew to stations where they could neither do harm nor suffer it.

Phips had thrown away nearly all his ammunition in this futile and disastrous attack, which should have been deferred till the moment when Walley, with his land force, had gained the rear of the town. Walley lay in his camp, his men wet, shivering with cold, famished, and sickening with the small-pox. Food, and all other supplies, were to have been brought him by the small vessels, which should have entered the mouth of the St. Charles and aided him to cross it. But he waited for them in vain. Every vessel that carried a gun had busied itself in cannonading, and the rest did not move. There appears to have been insubordination among the masters of these small craft, some of whom, being owners or part-owners of the vessels they commanded, were probably unwilling to run them into danger. Walley was no soldier; but he saw that to attempt the passage of the river without aid, under the batteries of the town and in the face of forces twice as numerous as his own, was not an easy task. Frontenac, on his part, says that he wished him to do so, knowing that the attempt would ruin him. The New England men were eager to push on; but the night of Thursday, the day of Phips's repulse, was so cold that ice formed more than an inch in thickness, and the half-starved militia suffered intensely. Six field-pieces, with their ammunition, had been sent ashore; but they were nearly useless, as there were no means of moving them. Half a barrel of musket powder, and one biscuit for each man, were also landed ; and with this meagre aid Walley was left to capture Quebec.   He might, had he dared, have made a dash across the ford on the morning of Thursday, and assaulted the town in the rear while Phips was cannonading it in front ; but his courage was not equal to so desperate a venture.   The firing ceased, and the possible opportunity was lost.   The citizen soldier despaired of success ; and, on the morning of Friday, he went on board the admiral's ship to explain his situation.   While he was gone, his men put themselves in motion, and advanced along the borders of the St. Charles towards the ford.   Frontenac, with three battalions of regular troops, went to receive them at the crossing ; while Sainte-Hélène, with his brother Longueuil, passed the ford with a body of Canadians, and opened fire on them from the neighboring thickets. Their advance parties were driven in, and there was a hot skirmish, the chief loss falling on the New England men, who were fully exposed.   On the side of the French, Sainte-Hélène was mortally wounded, and his brother was hurt by a spent ball.   Towards evening, the Canadians withdrew, and the English encamped for the night. Their commander presently rejoined them.   The admiral had given him leave to withdraw them to the fleet, and boats were accordingly sent to bring them off ; but, as these did not arrive till about daybreak, it was necessary to defer the embarkation till the next night.

At dawn, Quebec was all astir with the beating of drums and the ringing of bells.   The New England drums replied ; and Walley drew up his men under arms, expecting an attack, for the town was so near that the hubbub of voices from within could plainly be heard.   The noise gradually died away ; and, except a few shots from the ramparts, the invaders were left undisturbed. Walley sent two or three companies to beat up the neighboring thickets, where he suspected that the enemy was lurking. On the way, they had the good luck to find and kill a number of cattle, which they cooked and ate on the spot; whereupon, being greatly refreshed and invigorated, they dashed forward in complete disorder, and were soon met by the fire of the ambushed Canadians. Several more companies were sent to their support, and the skirmishing became lively. Three detachments from Quebec had crossed the river; and the militia of Beauport and Beaupré had hastened to join them. They fought like Indians, hiding behind trees or throwing themselves flat among the bushes, and laying repeated ambuscades as they slowly fell back. At length, they all made a stand on a hill behind the buildings and fences of a farm; and here they held their ground till night, while the New England men taunted them as cowards who would never fight except under cover.

Walley, who with his main body had stood in arms all day, now called in the skirmishers, and fell back to the landing-place, where, as soon as it grew dark, the boats arrived from the fleet. The sick men, of whom there were many, were sent on board, and then, amid floods of rain, the whole force embarked in noisy confusion, leaving behind them in the mud five of their cannon. Hasty as was their parting, their conduct on the whole had been creditable; and La Hontan, who was in Quebec at the time, says of them, "They fought vigorously, though as ill-disciplined as men gathered together at random could be; for they did not lack courage, and, if they failed, it was by reason of their entire ignorance of discipline, and because they were exhausted by the

fatigues of the voyage." Of Phips he speaks with
contempt, and says that he could not have served the
French better if they had bribed him to stand all the
while with his arms folded. Some allowance should,
nevertheless, be made him for the unmanageable character of the force under his command, the constitution
of which was fatal to military subordination.

On Sunday, the morning after the re-embarkation,
Phips called a council of officers, and it was resolved
that the men should rest for a day or two, that there
should be a meeting for prayer, and that, if ammunition
enough could be found, another landing should be at-
tempted; but the rough weather prevented the prayer-
meeting, and the plan of a new attack was fortunately
abandoned.

Quebec remained in agitation and alarm till Tuesday,
when Phips weighed anchor and disappeared, with all
his fleet, behind the Island of Orleans. He did not go
far, as indeed he could not, but stopped four leagues
below to mend rigging, fortify wounded masts, and stop
shot-holes. Subercase had gone with a detachment to
watch the retiring enemy; and Phips was repeatedly
seen among his men, on a scaffold at the side of his
ship, exercising his old trade of carpenter. This delay
was turned to good use by an exchange of prisoners.
Chief among those in the hands of the French was
Captain Davis, late commander at Casco Bay: and there
were also two young daughters of Lieutenant Clark, who
had been killed at the same place. Frontenac himself
had humanely ransomed these children from the Indians;
and Madame de Champigny, wife of the intendant, had,
with equal kindness, bought from them a little girl
named Sarah Gerrish, and placed her in charge of
the nuns at the Hôtel-Dieu, who had become greatly

attached to her, while she, on her part, left them with reluctance. The French had the better in these exchanges, receiving able-bodied men, and returning, with the exception of Davis, only women and children.

The heretics were gone, and Quebec breathed freely again. Her escape had been a narrow one; not that three thousand men, in part regular troops, defending one of the strongest positions on the continent, and commanded by Frontenac, could not defy the attacks of two thousand raw fishermen and farmers, led by an ignorant civilian, but the numbers which were a source of strength were at the same time a source of weakness. Nearly all the adult males of Canada were gathered at Quebec, and there was imminent danger of starvation. Cattle from the neighboring parishes had been hastily driven into the town; but there was little other provision, and before Phips retreated the pinch of famine had begun. Had he come a week earlier or stayed a week later, the French themselves believed that Quebec would have fallen, in the one case for want of men, and in the other for want of food.

Phips returned crestfallen to Boston late in November; and one by one the rest of the fleet came straggling after him, battered and weather-beaten. Some did not appear till February, and three or four never came at all. The autumn and early winter were unusually stormy. Captain Rainsford, with sixty men, was wrecked on the Island of Anticosti, where more than half their number died of cold and misery. In the other vessels, some were drowned, some frost-bitten, and above two hundred killed by small-pox and fever.

At Boston, all was dismay and gloom. The Puritan bowed before "this awful frown of God," and searched his conscience for the sin that had brought upon him so

stern a chastisement. Massachusetts, already impover-
ished, found herself in extremity. The war, instead of
paying for itself, had burdened her with an additional
debt of fifty thousand pounds. The sailors and soldiers
were clamorous for their pay; and, to satisfy them, the
colony was forced for the first time in its history to issue
a paper currency. It was made receivable at a premium
for all public debts, and was also fortified by a provision
for its early redemption by taxation; a provision which
was carried into effect in spite of poverty and distress.

Massachusetts had made her usual mistake. She had
confidently believed that ignorance and inexperience
could match the skill of a tried veteran, and that the
rude courage of her fishermen and farmers could triumph without discipline or leadership. The conditions
of her material prosperity were adverse to efficiency in
war. A trading republic, without trained officers, may
win victories; but it wins them either by accident or by
an extravagant outlay in money and life.

THE HEIGHTS OF ABRAHAM.

THE early part of the Seven Years' War was disastrous to England. The tide turned with the accession to power of the great war minister, William Pitt. In 1759, he sent General James Wolfe with a combined military and naval force to capture Quebec. The British troops numbered somewhat less than nine thousand, while Montcalm and Vaudreuil were posted to receive them, on positions almost impregnable, with an army of regulars, Canadians, and Indians, amounting in all to about sixteen thousand. The great height of the shores made the British ships of little or no use for purposes of attack.

Wolfe took possession of Point Levi, from which he bombarded Quebec. He also seized the high grounds just below the Montmorenci, and vainly tried to cross that stream above the cataract and gain the rear of Montcalm's army, which lay encamped along the shore from the Montmorenci to the city. Failing in this and every other attempt to force the enemy to a battle, he rashly resolved to attack them in front, up the steep declivities at the top of which they were intrenched. The grenadiers dashed forward prematurely and without orders, struggling desperately to scale the heights under a deadly fire. The result was a complete repulse, with heavy loss.

The capture of Quebec now seemed hopeless. Wolfe was almost in despair. His body was as frail as his

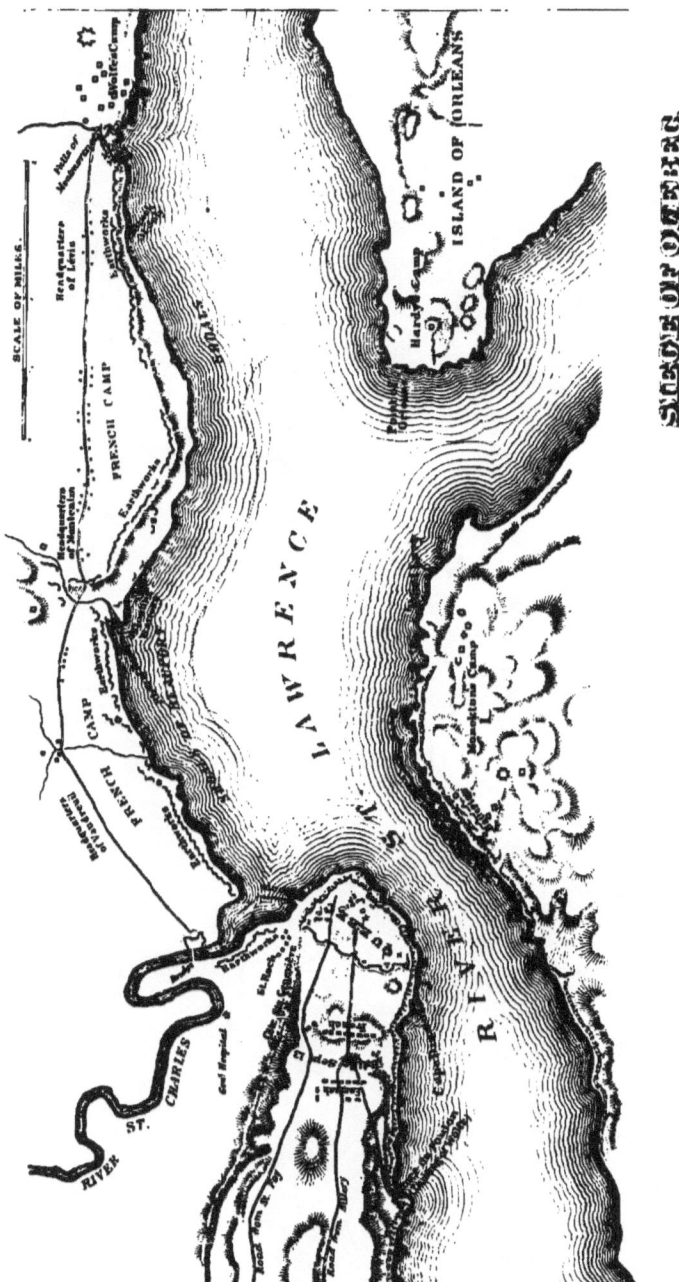

SIEGE OF QUEBEC.

1759.

spirit was ardent and daring. Since the siege began
he had passed with ceaseless energy from camp to
camp, animating the troops, observing everything,
and directing everything; but now the pale face and
tall lean form were seen no more, and the rumor spread
that the General was dangerously ill. He had in fact
been seized by an access of the disease that had tortured
him for some time past; and fever had followed. His
quarters were at a French farmhouse in the camp at
Montmorenci; and here, as he lay in an upper chamber,
helpless in bed, his singular and most unmilitary features haggard with disease and drawn with pain, no
man could less have looked the hero. But as the needle,
though quivering, points always to the pole, so, through
torment and languor and the heats of fever, the mind of
Wolfe dwelt on the capture of Quebec. His illness,
which began before the twentieth of August, had so
far subsided on the twenty-fifth that Captain Knox
wrote in his Diary of that day: "His Excellency General Wolfe is on the recovery, to the inconceivable joy
of the whole army." On the twenty-ninth he was able
to write or dictate a letter to the three brigadiers,
Monckton, Townshend, and Murray: "That the public
service may not suffer by the General's indisposition,
he begs the brigadiers will meet and consult together
for the public utility and advantage, and consider of the
best method to attack the enemy." The letter then
proposes three plans, all bold to audacity. The first
was to send a part of the army to ford the Montmorenci
eight or nine miles above its mouth, march through the
forest, and fall on the rear of the French at Beauport,
while the rest landed and attacked them in front. The
second was to cross the ford at the mouth of the Montmorenci and march along the strand, under the French

intrenchments, till a place could be found where the troops might climb the heights. The third was to make a general attack from boats at the Beauport flats. Wolfe had before entertained two other plans, one of which was to scale the heights at St. Michel, about a league above Quebec; but this he had abandoned on learning that the French were there in force to receive him. The other was to storm the Lower Town; but this also he had abandoned, because the Upper Town, which commanded it, would still remain inaccessible.

The brigadiers met in consultation, rejected the three plans proposed in the letter, and advised that an attempt should be made to gain a footing on the north shore above the town, place the army between Montcalm and his base of supply, and so force him to fight or surrender. The scheme was similar to that of the heights of St. Michel. It seemed desperate, but so did all the rest; and if by chance it should succeed, the gain was far greater than could follow any success below the town. Wolfe embraced it at once.

Not that he saw much hope in it. He knew that every chance was against him. Disappointment in the past and gloom in the future, the pain and exhaustion of disease, toils, and anxieties "too great," in the words of Burke, "to be supported by a delicate constitution, and a body unequal to the vigorous and enterprising soul that it lodged," threw him at times into deep dejection. By those intimate with him he was heard to say that he would not go back defeated, "to be exposed to the censure and reproach of an ignorant populace." In other moods he felt that he ought not to sacrifice what was left of his diminished army in vain conflict with hopeless obstacles. But his final resolve once taken, he would not swerve from it. His fear was that he might not be able to lead his troops in person. " I know perfectly well you cannot cure me," he said to his physician ; " but pray make me up so that I may be without pain for a few days, and able to do my duty : that is all I want."

On the last of August, he was able for the first time to leave the house. It was on this same day that he wrote his last letter to his mother : " My writing to you will convince you that no personal evils worse than defeats and disappointments have fallen upon me. The enemy puts nothing to risk, and I can't in conscience put the whole army to risk. My antagonist has wisely shut himself up in inaccessible intrenchments, so that I can't get at him without spilling a torrent of blood, and that perhaps to little purpose. The Marquis de Montcalm is at the head of a great number of bad soldiers, and I am at the head of a small number of good ones, that wish for nothing so much as to fight him ; but the wary old fellow avoids an action, doubtful of the behavior of his army. People must be of the profession to understand the disadvantages and difficulties we labor under, arising from the uncommon natural strength of the country."

On the second of September a vessel was sent to England with his last despatch to Pitt. It begins thus : " The obstacles we have met with in the operations of the campaign are much greater than we had reason to expect or could foresee ; not so much from the number of the enemy (though superior to us) as from the natural strength of the country, which the Marquis of Montcalm seems wisely to depend upon. When I learned that succors of all kinds had been thrown into Quebec ; that five battalions of regular troops, completed from the best inhabitants of the country, some of the troops of

the colony, and every Canadian that was able to bear
arms, besides several nations of savages, had taken the
field in a very advantageous situation, — I could not
flatter myself that I should be able to reduce the place.
I sought, however, an occasion to attack their army,
knowing well that with these troops I was able to fight,
and hoping that a victory might disperse them." Then,
after recounting the events of the campaign with ad-
mirable clearness, he continues : " I found myself so ill,
and am still so weak, that I begged the general officers
to consult together for the general utility. They are all
of opinion that, as more ships and provisions are now
got above the town, they should try, by conveying up
a corps of four or five thousand men (which is nearly
the whole strength of the army after the Points of Levi
and Orleans are left in a proper state of defence), to
draw the enemy from their present situation and bring
them to an action. I have acquiesced in the proposal,
and we are preparing to put it into execution." The letter ends thus : " By the list of disabled officers, many
of whom are of rank, you may perceive that the army is
much weakened. By the nature of the river, the most
formidable part of this armament is deprived of the
power of acting ; yet we have almost the whole force of
Canada to oppose. In this situation there is such a
choice of difficulties that I own myself at a loss how to
determine. The affairs of Great Britain, I know, require
the most vigorous measures ; but the courage of a hand-
ful of brave troops should be exerted only when there
is some hope of a favorable event ; however, you may
be assured that the small part of the campaign which
remains shall be employed, as far as I am able, for the
honor of His Majesty and the interest of the nation, in
which I am sure of being well seconded by the Admiral

and by the generals; happy if our efforts here can contribute to the success of His Majesty's arms in any other
parts of America."

Perhaps he was as near despair as his undaunted
nature was capable of being. In his present state of
body and mind he was a hero without the light and
cheer of heroism. He flattered himself with no illusions, but saw the worst and faced it all. He seems
to have been entirely without excitement. The languor
of disease, the desperation of the chances, and the great-
ness of the stake may have wrought to tranquillize him.
His energy was doubly tasked: to bear up his own
sinking frame, and to achieve an almost hopeless feat
of arms.

Audacious as it was, his plan cannot be called rash
if we may accept the statement of two well-informed
writers on the French side. They say that on the tenth
of September the English naval commanders held a
council on board the flagship, in which it was resolved
that the lateness of the season required the fleet to leave
Quebec without delay. They say further that Wolfe
then went to the Admiral, told him that he had found a
place where the heights could be scaled, that he would
send up a hundred and fifty picked men to feel the way,
and that if they gained a lodgment at the top, the other
troops should follow; if, on the other hand, the French
were there in force to oppose them, he would not sacrifice the army in a hopeless attempt, but embark them
for home, consoled by the thought that all had been
done that man could do. On this, concludes the story,
the Admiral and his officers consented to wait the
result.

As Wolfe had informed Pitt, his army was greatly
weakened. Since the end of June his loss in killed

and wounded was more than eight hundred and fifty, including two colonels, two majors, nineteen captains, and thirty-four subalterns; and to these were to be added a greater number disabled by disease.

The squadron of Admiral Holmes above Quebec had now increased to twenty-two vessels, great and small. One of the last that went up was a diminutive schooner, armed with a few swivels, and jocosely named the "Terror of France." She sailed by the town in broad daylight, the French, incensed at her impudence, blazing at her from all their batteries; but she passed unharmed, anchored by the Admiral's ship, and saluted him triumphantly with her swivels.

Wolfe's first move towards executing his plan was the critical one of evacuating the camp at Montmorenci. This was accomplished on the third of September. Montcalm sent a strong force to fall on the rear of the retiring English. Monckton saw the movement from Point Levi, embarked two battalions in the boats of the fleet, and made a feint of landing at Beauport. Montcalm recalled his troops to repulse the threatened attack; and the English withdrew from Montmorenci unmolested, some to the Point of Orleans, others to Point Levi. On the night of the fourth a fleet of flat boats passed above the town with the baggage and stores. On the fifth, Murray, with four battalions, marched up to the River Etechemin, and forded it under a hot fire from the French batteries at Sillery. Monckton and Townshend followed with three more battalions, and the united force, of about thirty-six hundred men, was embarked on board the ships of Holmes, where Wolfe joined them on the same evening.

These movements of the English filled the French commanders with mingled perplexity, anxiety, and hope.

A deserter told them that Admiral Saunders was impatient to be gone. Vaudreuil grew confident. "The breaking up of the camp at Montmorenci," he says, "and the abandonment of the intrenchments there, the re-embarkation on board the vessels above Quebec of the troops who had encamped on the south bank, the movements of these vessels, the removal of the heaviest pieces of artillery from the batteries of Point Levi,—these and the lateness of the season all combined to announce the speedy departure of the fleet, several vessels of which had even sailed down the river already. The prisoners and the deserters who daily came in told us that this was the common report in their army." He wrote to Bourlamaque on the first of September: "Everything proves that the grand design of the English has failed."

Yet he was ceaselessly watchful. So was Montcalm; and he, too, on the night of the second, snatched a moment to write to Bourlamaque from his headquarters in the stone house, by the river of Beauport: "The night is dark; it rains; our troops are in their tents, with clothes on, ready for an alarm; I in my boots; my horses saddled. In fact, this is my usual way. I wish you were here; for I cannot be everywhere, though I multiply myself, and have not taken off my clothes since the twenty-third of June." On the eleventh of September he wrote his last letter to Bourlamaque, and probably the last that his pen ever traced. "I am overwhelmed with work, and should often lose temper, like you, if I did not remember that I am paid by Europe for not losing it. Nothing new since my last. I give the enemy another month, or something less, to stay here." The more sanguine Vaudreuil would hardly give them a week.

11

Meanwhile, no precaution was spared. The force under Bougainville above Quebec was raised to three thousand men. He was ordered to watch the shore as far as Jacques-Cartier, and follow with his main body every movement of Holmes's squadron. There was little fear for the heights near the town; they were thought inaccessible. Even Montcalm believed them safe, and had expressed himself to that effect some time before. " We need not suppose," he wrote to Vaudreuil, " that the enemy have wings ; " and again, speaking of the very place where Wolfe afterwards landed, " I swear to you that a hundred men posted there would stop their whole army." He was right. A hundred watchful and determined men could have held the position long enough for reinforcements to come up.

The hundred men were there. Captain de Vergor, of the colony troops, commanded them, and reinforcements were within his call ; for the battalion of Guienne had been ordered to encamp close at hand on the Plains of Abraham. Vergor's post, called Anse du Foulon, was a mile and a half from Quebec. A little beyond it, by the brink of the cliffs, was another post, called Samos, held by seventy men with four cannon ; and, beyond this again, the heights of Sillery were guarded by a hundred and thirty men, also with cannon. These were outposts of Bougainville, whose headquarters were at Cap-Rouge, six miles above Sillery, and whose troops were in continual movement along the intervening shore. Thus all was vigilance ; for while the French were strong in the hope of speedy delivery, they felt that there was no safety till the tents of the invader had vanished from their shores and his ships from their river. " What we knew," says one of them, " of the character of M. Wolfe, that impetuous, bold, and intrepid warrior, prepared us for a last attack before he left us."

Wolfe had been very ill on the evening of the fourth. The troops knew it, and their spirits sank ; but, after a night of torment, he grew better, and was soon among them again, rekindling their ardor, and imparting a cheer that he could not share. For himself he had no pity ; but when he heard of the illness of two officers in one of the ships, he sent them a message of warm sympathy, advised them to return to Point Levi, and offered them his own barge and an escort. They thanked him, but replied that, come what might, they would see the enterprise to an end. Another officer remarked in his hearing that one of the invalids had a very delicate constitution. " Don't tell me of constitution," said Wolfe ; " he has good spirit, and good spirit will carry a man through everything." An immense moral force bore up his own frail body and forced it to its work.

Major Robert Stobo, who, five years before, had been given as a hostage to the French at the capture of Fort Necessity, arrived about this time in a vessel from Halifax. He had long been a prisoner at Quebec, not always in close custody, and had used his opportunities to acquaint himself with the neighborhood. In the spring of this year he and an officer of rangers named Stevens had made their escape with extraordinary skill and daring ; and he now returned to give his countrymen the benefit of his local knowledge. His biographer says that it was he who directed Wolfe in the choice of a landing-place. Be this as it may, Wolfe in person examined the river and the shores as far as Pointe-aux-Trembles ; till at length, landing on the south side a little above Quebec, and looking across the water with a telescope, he descried a path that ran with a long slope up the face of the woody precipice, and saw at the top a cluster of tents. They were those of Vergor's guard at the Anse du Foulon, now called Wolfe's Cove. As he could see but ten or twelve of them, he thought that the guard could not be numerous, and might be overpowered. His hope would have been stronger if he had known that Vergor had once been tried for misconduct and cowardice in the surrender of Beauséjour, and saved from merited disgrace by the friendship of the intendant Bigot, and the protection of Vaudreuil.

The morning of the seventh was fair and warm, and the vessels of Holmes, their crowded decks gay with scarlet uniforms, sailed up the river to Cap-Rouge. A lively scene awaited them ; for here were the headquarters of Bougainville, and here lay his principal force, while the rest watched the banks above and below. The cove into which the little river runs was guarded by floating batteries ; the surrounding shore was defended by breastworks ; and a large body of regulars, militia, and mounted Canadians in blue uniforms moved to and fro, with restless activity, on the hills behind. When the vessels came to anchor, the horsemen dismounted and formed in line with the infantry ; then, with loud shouts, the whole rushed down the heights to man their works at the shore. That true Briton, Captain Knox, looked on with a critical eye from the gangway of his ship, and wrote that night in his Diary that they had made a ridiculous noise. " How different ! " he exclaims, " how nobly awful and expressive of true valor is the customary silence of the British troops ! "

In the afternoon the ships opened fire, while the troops entered the boats and rowed up and down as if looking for a landing-place. It was but a feint of

Wolfe to deceive Bougainville as to his real design. A heavy easterly rain set in on the next morning, and lasted two days without respite. All operations were suspended, and the men suffered greatly in the crowded transports. Half of them were therefore landed on the south shore, where they made their quarters in the village of St. Nicolas, refreshed themselves, and dried their wet clothing, knapsacks, and blankets.

For several successive days the squadron of Holmes was allowed to drift up the river with the flood tide and down with the ebb, thus passing and repassing incessantly between the neighborhood of Quebec on one hand, and a point high above Cap-Rouge on the other; while Bougainville, perplexed, and always expecting an attack, followed the ships to and fro along the shore, by day and by night, till his men were exhausted with ceaseless forced marches.

At last the time for action came. On Wednesday, the twelfth, the troops at St. Nicolas were embarked again, and all were told to hold themselves in readiness. Wolfe, from the flagship " Sutherland," issued his last general orders. " The enemy's force is now divided, great scarcity of provisions in their camp, and universal discontent among the Canadians. Our troops below are in readiness to join us; all the light artillery and tools are embarked at the Point of Levi; and the troops will land where the French seem least to expect it. The first body that gets on shore is to march directly to the enemy and drive them from any little post they may occupy; the officers must be careful that the succeeding bodies do not by any mistake fire on those who go before them. The battalions must form on the upper ground with expedition, and be ready to charge whatever presents itself. When the artillery and troops are landed, a corps will be left to secure the landing-place, while the rest march on and endeavor to bring the Canadians and French to a battle. The officers and men will remember what their country expects from them, and what a determined body of soldiers inured to war is capable of doing against five weak French battalions mingled with a disorderly peasantry."

The spirit of the army answered to that of its chief. The troops loved and admired their general, trusted their officers, and were ready for any attempt. "Nay, how could it be otherwise," quaintly asks honest Sergeant John Johnson, of the fifty-eighth regiment, "being at the heels of gentlemen whose whole thirst, equal with their general, was for glory? We had seen them tried, and always found them sterling. We knew that they would stand by us to the last extremity."

Wolfe had thirty-six hundred men and officers with him on board the vessels of Holmes; and he now sent orders to Colonel Burton at Point Levi to bring to his aid all who could be spared from that place and the Point of Orleans. They were to march along the south bank, after nightfall, and wait further orders at a designated spot convenient for embarkation. Their number was about twelve hundred, so that the entire force destined for the enterprise was at the utmost forty-eight hundred. With these, Wolfe meant to climb the heights of Abraham in the teeth of an enemy who, though much reduced, were still twice as numerous as their assailants.

Admiral Saunders lay with the main fleet in the Basin of Quebec. This excellent officer, whatever may have been his views as to the necessity of a speedy departure, aided Wolfe to the last with unfailing energy and zeal. It was agreed between them that while the General

made the real attack, the Admiral should engage Montcalm's attention by a pretended one. As night approached, the fleet ranged itself along the Beauport
shore; the boats were lowered and filled with sailors,
marines, and the few troops that had been left behind;
while ship signalled to ship, cannon flashed and thundered, and shot ploughed the beach, as if to clear a
way for assailants to land. In the gloom of the evening
the effect was imposing. Montcalm, who thought that
the movements of the English above the town were only
a feint, that their main force was still below it, and that
their real attack would be made there, was completely
deceived, and massed his troops in front of Beauport to
repel the expected landing. But while in the fleet of
Saunders all was uproar and ostentatious menace, the
danger was ten miles away, where the squadron of
Holmes lay tranquil and silent at its anchorage off
Cap-Rouge.

It was less tranquil than it seemed. All on board
knew that a blow would be struck that night, though
only a few high officers knew where. Colonel Howe, of
the light infantry, called for volunteers to lead the unknown and desperate venture, promising, in the words
of one of them, "that if any of us survived we might
depend on being recommended to the General." As
many as were wanted — twenty-four in all — soon came
forward. Thirty large bateaux and some boats belonging to the squadron lay moored alongside the vessels;
and late in the evening the troops were ordered into
them, the twenty-four volunteers taking their place in
the foremost. They held in all about seventeen hundred
men. The rest remained on board.

Bougainville could discern the movement, and mis-
judged it, thinking that he himself was to be attacked.

The tide was still flowing; and, the better to deceive him, the vessels and boats were allowed to drift upward with it for a little distance, as if to land above Cap-Rouge.

The day had been fortunate for Wolfe. Two deserters came from the camp of Bougainville with intelligence that, at ebb tide on the next night, he was to send down a convoy of provisions to Montcalm. The necessities of the camp at Beauport, and the difficulties of transportation by land, had before compelled the French to resort to this perilous means of conveying supplies; and their boats, drifting in darkness under the shadows of the northern shore, had commonly passed in safety. Wolfe saw at once that, if his own boats went down in advance of the convoy, he could turn the intelligence of the deserters to good account.

He was still on board the "Sutherland." Every preparation was made, and every order given; it only remained to wait the turning of the tide. Seated with him in the cabin was the commander of the sloop-of-war "Porcupine," his former school-fellow John Jervis, afterwards Earl St. Vincent. Wolfe told him that he expected to die in the battle of the next day; and taking from his bosom a miniature of Miss Lowther, his betrothed, he gave it to him with a request that he would return it to her if the presentiment should prove true.

Towards two o'clock the tide began to ebb, and a fresh wind blew down the river. Two lanterns were raised into the maintop shrouds of the "Sutherland." It was the appointed signal; the boats cast off and fell down with the current, those of the light infantry leading the way. The vessels with the rest of the troops had orders to follow a little later.

To look for a moment at the chances on which this bold adventure hung. First, the deserters told Wolfe that provision-boats were ordered to go down to Quebec that night; secondly, Bougainville countermanded them; thirdly, the sentries posted along the heights were told of the order, but not of the countermand; fourthly, Vergor at the Anse du Foulon had permitted most of his men, chiefly Canadians from Lorette, to go home for a time and work at their harvesting, on condition, it is said, that they should afterwards work in a neighboring field of his own; fifthly, he kept careless watch, and went quietly to bed; sixthly, the battalion of Guienne, ordered to take post on the Plains of Abraham, had, for reasons unexplained, remained encamped by the St. Charles; and lastly, when Bougainville saw Holmes's vessels drift down the stream, he did not tax his weary troops to follow them, thinking that they would return as usual with the flood tide. But for these conspiring circumstances New France might have lived a little longer, and the fruitless heroism of Wolfe would have passed, with countless other heroisms, into oblivion.

For full two hours the procession of boats, borne on the current, steered silently down the St. Lawrence. The stars were visible, but the night was moonless and sufficiently dark. The General was in one of the foremost boats, and near him was a young midshipman, John Robison, afterwards professor of natural philosophy in the University of Edinburgh. He used to tell in his later life how Wolfe, with a low voice, repeated Gray's *Elegy in a Country Churchyard* to the officers about him. Probably it was to relieve the intense strain of his thoughts. Among the rest was the verse which his own fate was soon to illustrate, —

"The paths of glory lead but to the grave."

"Gentlemen," he said, as his recital ended, "I would rather have written those lines than take Quebec." None were there to tell him that the hero is greater than the poet.

As they neared their destination, the tide bore them in towards the shore, and the mighty wall of rock and forest towered in darkness on their left. The dead stillness was suddenly broken by the sharp *Qui vive !* of a French sentry, invisible in the thick gloom. *France !* answered a Highland officer of Fraser's regiment from one of the boats of the light infantry. He had served in Holland, and spoke French fluently.

À quel régiment ?

De la Reine, replied the Highlander. He knew that a part of that corps was with Bougainville. The sentry, expecting the convoy of provisions, was satisfied, and did not ask for the password.

Soon after, the foremost boats were passing the heights of Samos, when another sentry challenged them, and they could see him through the darkness running down to the edge of the water, within range of a pistol-shot. In answer to his questions, the same officer replied, in French: " Provision-boats. Don't make a noise ; the English will hear us." In fact, the sloop-of-war "Hunter" was anchored in the stream not far off. This time, again, the sentry let them pass. In a few moments they rounded the headland above the Anse du Foulon. There was no sentry there. The strong current swept the boats of the light infantry a little below the intended landing-place. They disembarked on a narrow strand at the foot of heights as steep as a hill covered with trees can be. The twenty-four volunteers led the way, climbing with what silence they might, closely followed by a much larger body. When they

reached the top they saw in the dim light a cluster of
tents at a short distance, and immediately made a dash
at them. Vergor leaped from bed and tried to run off,
but was shot in the heel and captured. His men, taken
by surprise, made little resistance. One or two were
caught, and the rest fled.

The main body of troops waited in their boats by the
edge of the strand. The heights near by were cleft by
a great ravine choked with forest trees; and in its
depths ran a little brook called Ruisseau St.-Denis,
which, swollen by the late rains, fell plashing in the
stillness over a rock. Other than this no sound could
reach the strained ear of Wolfe but the gurgle of the
tide and the cautious climbing of his advance-parties as
they mounted the steeps at some little distance from
where he sat listening. At length from the top came
a sound of musket-shots, followed by loud huzzas, and
he knew that his men were masters of the position.
The word was given ; the troops leaped from the boats
and scaled the heights, some here, some there, clutching
at trees and bushes, their muskets slung at their backs.
Tradition still points out the place, near the mouth of
the ravine, where the foremost reached the top. Wolfe
said to an officer near him : " You can try it, but I don't
think you'll get up." He himself, however, found
strength to drag himself up with the rest. The narrow
slanting path on the face of the heights had been made
impassable by trenches and abatis ; but all obstructions
were soon cleared away, and then the ascent was easy.
In the gray of the morning the long file of red-coated
soldiers moved quickly upward, and formed in order
on the plateau above.

Before many of them had reached the top, cannon
were heard close on the left. It was the battery at

Samos firing on the boats in the rear and the vessels descending from Cap-Rouge. A party was sent to silence it; this was soon effected, and the more distant battery at Sillery was next attacked and taken. As fast as the boats were emptied they returned for the troops left on board the vessels and for those waiting on the southern shore under Colonel Burton.

The day broke in clouds and threatening rain. Wolfe's battalions were drawn up along the crest of the heights. No enemy was in sight, though a body of Canadians had sallied from the town and moved along the strand towards the landing-place, whence they were quickly driven back. He had achieved the most critical part of his enterprise; yet the success that he coveted placed him in imminent danger. On one side was the garrison of Quebec and the army of Beauport, and Bougainville was on the other. Wolfe's alternative was victory or ruin; for if he should be overwhelmed by a combined attack, retreat would be hopeless. His feelings no man can know; but it would be safe to say that hesitation or doubt had no part in them.

He went to reconnoitre the ground, and soon came to the Plains of Abraham, so called from Abraham Martin, a pilot known as Maître Abraham, who had owned a piece of land here in the early times of the colony. The Plains were a tract of grass, tolerably level in most parts, patched here and there with corn-fields, studded with clumps of bushes, and forming a part of the high plateau at the eastern end of which Quebec stood. On the south it was bounded by the declivities along the St. Lawrence; on the north, by those along the St. Charles, or rather along the mead-ows through which that lazy stream crawled like a

writhing snake. At the place that Wolfe chose for
his battle-field the plateau was less than a mile
wide.

Thither the troops advanced, marched by files till
they reached the ground, and then wheeled to form their
line of battle, which stretched across the plateau and
faced the city. It consisted of six battalions and the
detached grenadiers from Louisbourg, all drawn up in
ranks three deep. Its right wing was near the brink
of the heights along the St. Lawrence; but the left
could not reach those along the St. Charles. On this
side a wide space was perforce left open, and there was
danger of being outflanked. To prevent this, Brigadier
Townshend was stationed here with two battalions,
drawn up at right angles with the rest, and fronting the
St. Charles. The battalion of Webb's regiment, under
Colonel Burton, formed the reserve; the third battalion
of Royal Americans was left to guard the landing; and
Howe's light infantry occupied a wood far in the rear.
Wolfe, with Monckton and Murray, commanded the
front line, on which the heavy fighting was to fall, and
which, when all the troops had arrived, numbered less
than thirty-five hundred men.

Quebec was not a mile distant, but they could not
see it; for a ridge of broken ground intervened, called
Buttes-à-Neveu, about six hundred paces off. The first
division of troops had scarcely come up when, about six
o'clock, this ridge was suddenly thronged with white
uniforms. It was the battalion of Guienne, arrived at
the eleventh hour from its camp by the St. Charles.
Some time after there was hot firing in the rear. It
came from a detachment of Bougainville's command
attacking a house where some of the light infantry were
posted. The assailants were repulsed, and the firing

ceased. Light showers fell at intervals, besprinkling the troops as they stood patiently waiting the event.

Montcalm had passed a troubled night. Through all the evening the cannon bellowed from the ships of Saunders, and the boats of the fleet hovered in the dusk off the Beauport shore, threatening every moment to land. Troops lined the intrenchments till day, while the General walked the field that adjoined his head-quarters till one in the morning, accompanied by the Chevalier Johnstone and Colonel Poulariez. Johnstone says that he was in great agitation, and took no rest all night. At daybreak he heard the sound of cannon above the town. It was the battery at Samos firing on the English ships. He had sent an officer to the quarters of Vaudreuil, which were much nearer Quebec, with orders to bring him word at once should anything unusual happen. But no word came, and about six o'clock he mounted and rode thither with Johnstone. As they advanced, the country behind the town opened more and more upon their sight; till at length, when opposite Vaudreuil's house, they saw across the St. Charles, some two miles away, the red ranks of British soldiers on the heights beyond.

"This is a serious business," Montcalm said; and sent off Johnstone at full gallop to bring up the troops from the centre and left of the camp. Those of the right were in motion already, doubtless by the Governor's order. Vaudreuil came out of the house. Montcalm stopped for a few words with him; then set spurs to his horse, and rode over the bridge of the St. Charles to the scene of danger. He rode with a fixed look, uttering not a word.

The army followed in such order as it might, crossed the bridge in hot haste, passed under the northern rampart of Quebec, entered at the Palace Gate, and pressed on in headlong march along the quaint narrow streets of the warlike town : troops of Indians in scalplocks and war-paint, a savage glitter in their deep-set eyes ; bands of Canadians whose all was at stake, — faith, country, and home ; the colony regulars ; the battalions of Old France, a torrent of white uniforms and gleaming bayonets, La Sarre, Languedoc, Roussillon, Béarn, — victors of Oswego, William Henry, and Ticonderoga. So they swept on. poured out upon the plain, some by the gate of St. Louis, and some by that of St John, and hurried, breathless, to where the banners of Guienne still fluttered on the ridge.

Montcalm was amazed at what he saw. He had expected a detachment, and he found an army. Full in sight before him stretched the lines of Wolfe : the close ranks of the English infantry, a silent wall of red, and the wild array of the Highlanders, with their waving tartans, and bagpipes screaming defiance. Vaudreuil had not come ; but not the less was felt the evil of a divided authority and the jealousy of the rival chiefs. Montcalm waited long for the forces he had ordered to join him from the left wing of the army. He waited in vain. It is said that the Governor had detained them, lest the English should attack the Beauport shore. Even if they did so, and succeeded, the French might defy them, could they but put Wolfe to rout on the Plains of Abraham. Neither did the garrison of Quebec come to the aid of Montcalm. He sent to Ramesay, its commander, for twenty-five field-pieces which were on the Palace battery. Ramesay would give him only three. saying that he wanted them for his own defence. There were orders and counter-orders ; misunderstanding, haste, delay, perplexity.

Montcalm and his chief officers held a council of war. It is said that he and they alike were for immediate attack. His enemies declare that he was afraid lest Vaudreuil should arrive and take command; but the Governor was not a man to assume responsibility at such a crisis. Others say that his impetuosity overcame his better judgment; and of this charge it is hard to acquit him. Bougainville was but a few miles distant, and some of his troops were much nearer; a messenger sent by way of Old Lorette could have reached him in an hour and a half at most, and a combined attack in front and rear might have been concerted with him. If, moreover, Montcalm could have come to an understanding with Vaudreuil, his own force might have been strengthened by two or three thousand additional men from the town and the camp of Beauport; but he felt that there was no time to lose, for he imagined that Wolfe would soon be reinforced, which was impossible, and he believed that the English were fortifying themselves, which was no less an error. He has been blamed not only for fighting too soon, but for fighting at all. In this he could not choose. Fight he must, for Wolfe was now in a position to cut off all his supplies. His men were full of ardor, and he resolved to attack before their ardor cooled. He spoke a few words to them in his keen, vehement way. "I remember very well how he looked," one of the Canadians, then a boy of eighteen, used to say in his old age; "he rode a black or dark bay horse along the front of our lines, brandishing his sword, as if to excite us to do our duty. He wore a coat with wide sleeves, which fell back as he raised his arm, and showed the white linen of the wristband."

The English waited the result with a composure which,

if not quite real, was at least well feigned. The three field-pieces sent by Ramesay plied them with canister-shot, and fifteen hundred Canadians and Indians fusilladed them in front and flank. Over all the plain, from behind bushes and knolls and the edge of cornfields, puffs of smoke sprang incessantly from the guns of these hidden marksmen. Skirmishers were thrown out before the lines to hold them in check, and the soldiers were ordered to lie on the grass to avoid the shot. The firing was liveliest on the English left, where bands of sharp-shooters got under the edge of the declivity, among thickets, and behind scattered houses, whence they killed and wounded a considerable number of Townshend's men. The light infantry were called up from the rear. The houses were taken and retaken, and one or more of them was burned.

Wolfe was everywhere. How cool he was, and why his followers loved him, is shown by an incident that happened in the course of the morning. One of his captains was shot through the lungs; and on recovering consciousness he saw the General standing at his side. Wolfe pressed his hand, told him not to despair, praised his services, promised him early promotion, and sent an aide-de-camp to Monckton to beg that officer to keep the promise if he himself should fall.

It was towards ten o'clock when, from the high ground on the right of the line, Wolfe saw that the crisis was near. The French on the ridge had formed themselves into three bodies, regulars in the centre, regulars and Canadians on right and left. Two field-pieces, which had been dragged up the heights at Anse du Foulon, fired on them with grape-shot, and the troops, rising from the ground, prepared to receive them. In a few moments more they were in motion. They came

12

on rapidly, uttering loud shouts, and firing as soon as they were within range. Their ranks, ill ordered at the best, were further confused by a number of Canadians who had been mixed among the regulars, and who, after hastily firing, threw themselves on the ground to reload. The British advanced a few rods ; then halted and stood still. When the French were within forty paces the word of command rang out, and a crash of musketry answered all along the line. The volley was delivered with remarkable precision. In the battalions of the centre, which had suffered least from the enemy's bullets, the simultaneous explosion was afterwards said by French officers to have sounded like a cannon-shot. Another volley followed, and then a furious clattering fire that lasted but a minute or two. When the smoke rose, a miserable sight was revealed : the ground cumbered with dead and wounded, the advancing masses stopped short and turned into a frantic mob, shouting, cursing, gesticulating. The order was given to charge. Then over the field rose the British cheer, mixed with the fierce yell of the Highland slogan. Some of the corps pushed forward with the bayonet ; some advanced firing. The clansmen drew their broadswords and dashed on, keen and swift as bloodhounds. At the English right, though the attacking column was broken to pieces, a fire was still kept up, chiefly, it seems, by sharpshooters from the bushes and cornfields, where they had lain for an hour or more. Here Wolfe himself led the charge, at the head of the Louisbourg grenadiers. A shot shattered his wrist. He wrapped his handkerchief about it and kept on. Another shot struck him, and he still advanced, when a third lodged in his breast. He staggered, and sat on the ground. Lieutenant Brown, of the grenadiers, one Henderson, a vol-

unteer in the same company, and a private soldier, aided
by an officer of artillery who ran to join them, carried
him in their arms to the rear. He begged them to lay
him down. They did so, and asked if he would have a
surgeon. "There's no need," he answered; "it's all
over with me." A moment after, one of them cried
out: "They run; see how they run!" "Who run?"
Wolfe demanded, like a man roused from sleep. "The
enemy, sir. Egad, they give way everywhere!" "Go,
one of you, to Colonel Burton," returned the dying man;
"tell him to march Webb's regiment down to Charles
River, to cut off their retreat from the bridge." Then,
turning on his side, he murmured, "Now, God be praised,
I will die in peace!" and in a few moments his gallant
soul had fled.

Montcalm, still on horseback, was borne with the tide
of fugitives towards the town. As he approached the
walls a shot passed through his body. He kept his seat;
two soldiers supported him, one on each side, and led
his horse through the St. Louis Gate. On the open
space within, among the excited crowd, were several
women, drawn, no doubt, by eagerness to know the
result of the fight. One of them recognized him,
saw the streaming blood, and shrieked, "*O mon Dieu!
mon Dieu! le Marquis est tué!*" "It's nothing, it's
nothing," replied the death-stricken man; "don't be
troubled for me, my good friends." ("*Ce n'est rien, ce
n'est rien; ne vous affligez pas pour moi, mes bonnes
amies.*")

Some of the fugitives took refuge in the city and
others escaped across the St. Charles. In the next
night the French army abandoned Quebec to its fate
and fled up the St. Lawrence. The city soon surren-

dered to Wolfe's successor, Brigadier Townshend, and the English held it during the winter. In April, the French under the Chevalier de Lévis made a bold but unsuccessful attempt to retake it. In the following summer, General Amherst advanced on Montreal, till in September all Canada was forced to surrender, and the power of France was extinguished on the North American continent.